C.S. Boag

MISTER RAINBOW

in the Case of the

HOOD WITH NO HANDS

XOUM PUBLISHING

Sydney

By the same author

The Case of the Death of a Ladies' Man

The Case of the Horses for Corpses

For Beth, Zan, Stew, Jack and Kate

Chapter 1

RENDEZVOUS WITH A DAME

The name's Rainbow.

You can spit on my card, bend it, twist it, rub it with your shirt sleeve or blast a hole through it with a .38, it will still read: Bruno Scutt's Detective Agency, brunscutt.etcetera.com and down the bottom the catchy little phrase:

'No Care Taken, But All Responsibility'.

Means as much as anything these days.

Whatever it says, I'm still Rainbow.

The card's so I look respectable.

No matter that I live on a boat, crappy little number, grubs munching their way through the hull, engine a lottery, only thing functions is the automatic bilge pump, gizmo that squirts out the water just that bit faster than it comes in and keeps me out of the teeth of sharks.

So does getting cash up front.

Might sound like I don't trust people.

Might be right.

So when this dame responds to my ad in the Personals of *The Sydney Morning Horrible*, that well-known navel-gazing bastion of political correctness tacked onto the only good thing about the rag – the comics – that's the first thing I ask her.

Not how long have you been suspicious of your husband or are you seeking a short-term relationship with a private detective aged forty-five, no ties he'll admit to except the ones he gets at op shops, suspicious of aliens, but prepared to walk barefoot on beaches in the moonlight, if that's what it takes.

None of that.

Not straight up, anyhow.

No, when she telephones and asks in the echoey sort of voice that can only come out of a bomb shelter in Beirut or an ancient telephone booth in an Australian country town if I can check up on her old man, I tell her only if she produces the requisite number of dollars at a reasonably early stage in the proceedings, like immediately after the Hello-I'm-Bruno bit.

That's how I find myself in Dashiell, a biggish and crappy-enough rural proclivity in NSW's west, lurking under a Cinzano umbrella in a caffeine-den next to a funeral parlour on a coolish morning in March, battered Panama on the table before me, gulping down my third triple-shot for the day and reading the pulps, in this case the flirty-and-dirty women's magazines, as provided by a socially responsible management.

I'm just learning how I can keep my fanny in shape when up she slopes, in that tentatively confident manner peculiar to seriously beautiful women, the greatest knockout since Buster Douglas floored Mike Tyson in anno Domini 1990 – tall, willowy, blonde and about as born-to-rule as John F. Kennedy, before he was assassinated.

'Mr Scutt? I'm Sally Kane.'

Pale-grey pantsuit, pale-grey eyes to match the pantsuit, aristocratic stoop; it's like Sally Kane has spent her whole life trying to descend to the level of ordinary mortals; and the hand in mine is like something out of a waxworks.

I look at her inquiringly – that is, with the head to one side and the left eyebrow raised, never having perfected the right eyebrow lift, although God knows I've tried.

'Of course,' she says, letting go my paw and reaching into her bag, a monster of a thing with Gucci and pure class written all over it, hauling out a smaller bag of the brown-paper variety with nothing on it but promises, 'the money.'

The straw-haired character second table from the left glances our way, as does the dame wearing nothing but star-spangled swimmers and goose-bumps selling red roses out of a cigarette tray, but I bring the loot up to my face, sniff at it like it's lunch, and stuff the dough-re-you down the front of my schnauzers.

'Best not do too much in the way of advertising.'

'I'm sorry.'

Sweet voice, all rounded vowels and rolled r's and an even sweeter manner about her.

'It's okay,' I tell her, 'but don't do it again.'

Waiter hovering.

Could only happen in an Australian country town.

Sally Kane requests a skinny latte, I order yet another black-as-night zinger, and when the boy finally wanders off I turn the magnetism of my bloodshot eyes upon her.

'So what can I do you for?'

'It's my husband.'

Well, I want to say, I know it's your bloody husband, but it's her time and she's paying, so all I say is, 'What's he done, this husband of yours?'

'That's just it. He hasn't done anything.'

It's okay, I tell myself, I've got the dough.

'Right.' I drag the notebook and biro that were on special in the two-dollar shop at Newtown out of the side pocket of my Vinnies jacket and write, *Husband does nothing*, before looking back at her perched on the other side of the table with an anxious expression on her dial-up. 'And you don't like him doing nothing?'

The waiter deposits our coffees and Madame Kane colours.

'I'm sorry,' she says again, 'I – I'm not used to this.'

'Okay, why don't we start with the basics. What's his name?'

'David Jones. As in the department store.'

I write it down, looks professional.

'Address?'

She tells me the address: 48 Daisy Drive.

'And you're married to this joker?'

'Yes.'

'How long have you known him?'

'Six years come February.'

'Happy marriage?'

'I – guess so.'

Hit a sore thumb, mine if not hers.

'There are different kinds of happy. What kind was yours?'

I say *was*, it's instinctive. In my experience all happy marriages end up in the past. But if she notices, it doesn't show. Instead she answers the question. They've been married five years and the whole thing's amiable enough. He puts out the garbage, there's money to buy the groceries and they don't argue.

'So what happened?'

I busy myself writing. Always relaxes them. *Top up mobiles. Buy Dettol for shaving. Bail out bilge.*

'It was as though . . .' She says *as though*, not *like*, I like that. '. . . he had been getting sick over a long period and I hadn't noticed until one day it hit me that something must be – awfully wrong.' She leans forward. 'There was something inside him, like some sort of growth, and on this particular day it struck him, and he became – even quieter.'

'A woman's intuition?'

'I would like to think,' she says, 'that it was an informed judgment.'

I write, *Attitude.*

'Anything else?'

'You don't think what I'm saying is enough. You want to know why it matters now.'

I shrug.

'All right, it's because I want to have a baby. But first' – she takes a deep breath – 'I need to know the true identity of the father.'

I write, *Biological time-bomb*, then glance up.

She's still beautiful.

'So what's he look like, this husband of yours?'

'Medium height' – she shoots me a glance – 'shorter than you, certainly. Symmetrical features. And again, unlike you – if you don't mind my saying so – handsome in a traditional sort of way. And there's a . . . restiveness about him, a wariness – as though he thinks he's being followed.'

I write, *Paranoid.*

'Employment?'

'He's an estate agent.' Then, like the job needs brushing up a bit, as a vocation, 'it's his own business.'

'Do you work?'

'Yes.'

'And what kind of work might that be?'

A little clothing store. She'd be right at home behind a counter. Or a volunteer with Vinnies, helping the underprivileged, because her husband can afford it. Or an assistant to a dentist. Those hands.

'I'm a – surgeon,' she says. 'Neuro.'

And then she looks behind her.

Chapter 2

THE MAN WITH NO PAST

But it's only the star-spangled dame selling red roses – except it's noses not roses and she's giving them away not flogging them – leaning down to say she hopes our stay in Dashiell will be a pleasant one and we'll visit the circus when it comes to town. She says it so nice that I take one of her schnozzles and palm it across to Sally Kane, who rolls it around the table for a couple of laps before tucking it into a pocket and telling me all she knows, which is nine-tenths of nothing.

They meet, they fall in love, they get married. Only they don't live happily ever after. On account of he's got no background.

I stop taking notes.

'What do you mean "no background"?'

She tells me what she means. David Jones's life began when he first met Sally Kane. He didn't talk about his past and she didn't ask. She got the impression he'd had a Struggletown childhood and he was naturally reluctant to talk about it. He was also something of a mechanical genius.

I don't tell her straight up, but my bet is another woman, possibly another wife, who one day appears out of the wide-blue azure to discover David Jones is double-dipping on her and decides to climb into him for a cut. It would make anyone go quiet.

'When he does talk, how's he sound? Drop his haitches? Say anythink? End his sentences with but? Talk like me, for example?'

Sally Kane takes a sip of her coffee. Doesn't gulp. Brain surgeon. 'No, nothing like that.' She dabs at her mouth with a serviette. 'David has what I would call perfect intonation.'

After half an hour I still don't get it. Might be a battler but talks good. Might not be a battler but he's got a past to hide. I pocket the notebook. All that money in my jock but I've still got to earn it.

'So what's the problem? He does the washing-up. Makes not as much as you do but still quite a bundle. Talks nice. And he's not playing around with teenagers. What's to complain about?'

She shakes her beautiful locks. 'Mr Scutt, you would have been to the theatre?'

I shrug. I might have attended the odd performance.

'Then you'll know how easy it is to be fooled.' She folds the serviette and turns her eyes on mine. 'That is, of course, if you want to be.'

I inspect my chapeau. There's a hole in the crown and the brim's torn.

'Look,' she says. 'I spent a long time studying. After school I did three years of Arts, majoring in psychology, followed by five years for my medical degree, then specialisation. No diversions.'

'None?'

'None. I was nearly thirty before I looked at a man who didn't need something doing to his brain.'

I take a swig of my coffee.

'Meanwhile, the hospital was having these meetings about its facilities, or the lack of them.' She fiddles with the salt. 'They were looking at property and David was in property. I met him at one of our meetings. I was thirty. I wanted to be fooled.'

'And he fooled you?'

Again the colouring. Brain surgeon with the emotional age of a schoolgirl.

'I – I don't know.' Again that hesitation. 'All I know is that I'm thirty-five now and want to have a baby.'

And would like to know who the father is. Or is going to be.

'So you decided to hire a private detective to check out your husband's bona fides before entering into a state of parenthood with him.'

She hunches her beautiful shoulders and says something.

Her head's down and it's hard to hear so I ask her to repeat it and this time I manage to catch the answer.

'Please, I – I don't like doing this. Also, I don't want him to know about it.' Her voice is barely a whisper, like she doesn't want anyone else to know about it either. 'Do you understand, Mr Bruno – I'm sorry – Scutt?'

'Yeah.' The joker with the straw-coloured hair doesn't look up as I leave and the perfume on the dame in the swimmers smells of candy-stripe.

Chapter 3

THE DAME GETS COLD FEET

Detecting's a case of following the trail, like the babes with the breadcrumbs in the fairy story. Only trouble is, after six years there aren't many breadcrumbs left in the forest.

After I've done the train ride and the bus trip and rowed myself back to the boat, I climb aboard the *Wooden No*. She's struggling to stay afloat in its hidey-hole in Sydney Harbour, an old tub with no identifying marks on its hull bar the forged code and the bit of rough patching where she crashed into wharf number six on grand final day 1987, ghosts of passengers past wandering the wraparound decks, an overworked bilge pump, and a pair of kamikaze seagulls that have set up home in the wheelhouse. I call her the *Wooden No* so that when nosy parkers ask what she's called I can just tell them 'Wooden No'.

I like my privacy.

All right, I got a business card but business cards can say anything, which is pretty much what mine says.

For the rest, I got no phone of my own, no bank account, no driver's licence, my marriage wasn't really a marriage, Aunt Rube got my birth expunged from the records, emails come to the account of a dead man, and my address when I've got one's a boat. It doesn't make me the invisible man, but it does make it that much harder for jokers to find me.

I fight my way past the empty-nesters, disentangle the Toshiba from the fingerprint powder and the secret-ink solvent and the mini-cam and the rest of the paraphernalia pertaining to detecting, plant the mainframe among the flotsam on the map table, and dial up Natality, Mortality and

Misery Inc, also known as the Department of Births, Deaths and Marriages.

Everything starts with Births, Deaths and Marriages.

That's where you're most likely to find the breadcrumbs.

There are thirty million one hundred thousand Joneses on Google, six hundred and forty-nine thousand when you narrow it down to the Land of Oz, and even after you chuck in the prenom 'David', subtract thirty-eight to get a birth year and put in a couple of half-baked applications using Sally Kane's survival rations, there's still too many babes in the wood.

A vessel ploughs past and the boat rocks.

As you age you acquire presbyopia.

Nothing to do with religion and everything to do with long sight, which is why you see so many codgers holding *The Sydney Morning Horrible* at arm's length in public libraries in the vain hope of making some sense of their increasingly confusing lives.

I mightn't be able to delineate my toenails but I can see what they've done to the name.

While the vessel might once have been called *Bullet*, now it's *Ballet*.

One word over another.

Aunt Rube would have called it a palimpsest.

The mobiles are all out of credit so I take off the plimsolls, roll up the schnauzers, climb into the dinghy, row to the nearest patch of shingle, dig out some shrapnel, find a public phone that works, and dial up the digits.

'Dr Kane?'

'No, this is Reception.'

Reception's got a rising inflection.

'I wish to speak to Dr Kane.'

'I'm sorry but S. Kane is listed under surgeon so that would make it Mr Kane.'

I let Reception have it her way and finally get put through to Sally Kane.

'Scutt here.'

'Oh, yes, Mr Scutt.'

I imagine Sally Kane covering the speaker tube with one of her beautiful hands. Brain surgeons don't consult private detectives. They don't have private lives to consult private detectives about. Like the Queen they probably don't even go to the toilet.

'It's difficult to talk just now.'

Forty cents left. Says so in the little window.

'Look, I just need to get a handle on this husband of yours. David Jones could be an invention. He ever call himself anything else?'

Sally Kane's ready with her answer. 'His driver's licence says David Jones, all accounts are in both our names – again it's David Jones – and no one calls and asks for anyone called Freddie.'

That answers most of my question.

'I need to see him.'

'And tell him I hired you?'

'He won't know a thing.'

'Mr Scutt?'

Twenty cents left.

'Yeah?'

'Oh, I don't know, it all seems so – wrong.'

'What does?'

'This – spying business.'

Ten cents left.

'Look, lady, we just need to find out if your Mr Jones is who he says he is. If it turns out he is then everything's fresh cream straight from the cow, if not –'

But our time's up and so is my money. I get myself back to the smack, push it off the shingle, row back to the *Wooden No* and climb aboard, my body on deck but my mind off in Neverland. I'm just starting to pack the overnight for a return trip to Dashiell when the Port Jackson Jazz Band breaks into *Hot Nights in Hawaii*.

Chapter 4

ALWAYS CALL
THEM DARLING

The racket's coming from the pile of mobiles in the bilge and I finally locate the offender – Phone No. 7, the Sony-Payola – and hit the little red button to shut it up, but when the music restarts I accidentally thump the little green handset instead.

'Is that Mr Rainbow?'

A bill collector or the taxation department or a pal of Pandora's.

'No.'

'Have you got another name now, Daddy?'

A kid.

One of mine.

'Sorry, darling.'

Always call them darling.

That way you can't get the name wrong.

'You forgot your name, didn't you, Daddy. But you didn't forget the circus as well, did you?'

'What circus?'

Silence.

I don't like silences, not from anyone, but especially not from kids.

'You still there, darling?'

'When you took me to Red Rooster I was playing with one of your mobiles, remember? And you promised to take me to the circus if I gave it back to you so I gave it back to you.'

Pause.

I figure the kid's fighting back tears.

'It's the last day before they go to the country and they've got this clown in it and . . .'

I taste citrus.

'Look, darling,' I tell her, 'it's just that I'm on this case, see, and . . .'

More silence at the other end of the cellophane.

Kids are like humans. You break an appointment, they send you a bill. Only with kids the bill's an emotional one.

'Darling?'

'You promised me, Daddy.'

'Look, Sophie, I'm real sorry, but it's work and I . . .'

No reply.

'Sophie?'

'It's not Sophie, it's Imogene.' Then she hangs up.

My hands are shaking as I climb back up on deck only to discover that the zip on the overnight bag won't work because the salt air has fused the alloy, but also because my fingers have turned into thumbs and my muscles to jelly.

I'd ring the kid back, only all my accounts are running on empty.

I'm probably a bit low on credit with Imogene, too.

I pick up the bag and lug it to the diving board, tripping over a hawser on the way.

My eyes aren't seeing so good.

And it's not presbyopia.

Chapter 5

A NICE LITTLE LIFESTYLE

Dashiell's 'Jones, Jones and Jones, the Realtors You Can Trust' are situated just up from the barber's, Woolworths, a gentlemen's outfitter, an op shop for the underprivileged, a boutique for the spouses of solicitors, an apothecary, a funeral parlour, and the caff where I first met Sally Kane.

I pause to examine the Vaseline-smeared images of desirable properties in the window but all I see is the reflection of a joker wearing a hat that looks like it's been savaged by a pack of dingoes, fists jammed deep in his pockets, and a gormless expression on his phyzog.

Reflections are always of this joker when they should be of me.

I head back to the outfitters where for eight slices of Dr Kane's homespun I'm sold a pink shirt with white detachable collar, a set of hot-burgundy cufflinks in the shape of tommy-guns, a pink tie, red braces, a pair of orange-and-white brogues, a pale-green fedora with a feather in the side, plus a yellow-check bag of fruit with an iridescent fleck in it.

While I'm waiting for the waist adjustment, I duck into the leech's for a haircut.

The facial and haircut take half an hour per itemo and set Dr Kane back another fifty clams but it's money well misspent because after I've packed myself into the shirt, the bag of fruit, the headwear and the shoes and got myself back to the dream flogger's, the image might still be of some other guy but now it's a guy who's had a haircut and facial and whose schnauzers don't bunch over his stogies.

The receptionist at Jones, Jones and Jones, the Realtors

You Can Trust is a chirpy little number who might once have handed me over to 'Rentals' but now on account of the makeover decides I might just make it into 'Sales'.

She's armed with a telephone, a glass paperweight with fairies in it, and a vase of what might be nasturtiums.

'Good morning,' she says in a voice that's almost as bright as the flowers, 'would you be Industrial, Residential or Acreage?'

I nod the new coif.

Her face says: The customer's always right.

'We'll put down all three.' She busies herself with a ball-point decorated with a plastic replica of a yeti, on the end that's not used for writing. 'Name?'

I tell her a name.

'Very well, Mr Brown, now if you'd just take a seat, Mr Jones or Mr Jones will be with you shortly.'

I'm busy looking at the images of desirable properties plus the accompanying price tags and trying to figure how the two fit together when out trots Jones, looking pretty much like Sally Kane said he would.

'Mr Brown?' He holds out a paw. 'Very nice to meet you.'

We do the handshake thing and the How-are-you? thing after which he slips me his business card, takes me into his equally neat office, casts a connoisseur's eye over the papyrus the receptionist palmed him, nods, and consults his computer.

'How many Joneses are there?' I ask by way of conversation.

He keeps his panhandle on the computer. 'Several million, I believe.'

Those well-modulated tones and nice articulation that Sally Kane told me about.

'I mean here.'

'In this firm?'

'Yeah.'

'Just the one.' He brings his eyes back to me, the sort of eyes you'd want to buy property from. 'How many were you expecting?'

I keep the voice steady and the face as bland as a pizza base.

'Well, your business name suggests there might be several and your receptionist –'

'Ah, my receptionist . . .'

'– said that Mr Jones *or* Mr Jones would be with me shortly.'

Jones laughs just as shortly.

'It's our little joke, but also the suggestion of more than one principal implies stability, reliability and trustworthiness, don't you think?' He looks at me keenly before going back to his computer. 'But we're not here to discuss people's names, are we?'

I tell him No, we're not here to discuss people's names, so we discuss what we might be here for and after that Jones gets off his stool and I take a final shooftee around his office and Jones checks the street both ways plus one more time for good measure as we leave the premises, after which we climb into his nice, neat realtor's limo and hit the road.

Jones shows me a block of flats with cracks in it, a decommissioned Episcopalian church, and – just this side of a hill which I note possesses a little white cottage on the other side of it – a hobby farm that looks more hobby than farm, containing a driveway, a plough, a bunch of wombat holes, a couple of weather-beaten chooks, the odd gum tree, several acres of dust, and a shack.

'Nice little lifestyle farm.'

They got a language all their own, these realtors.

He waves a paw in the direction of the shack.

Its roof looks like a much-patched tyre, with a bunch of black squares all over it.

'They're solar panels,' he explains, like it's yet another of the joint's irresistible features. 'They don't feed into the grid, so you're not at the mercy of broken political promises, and although you run out of power when it's cloudy, the things are unbeatable when it's fine.'

Back at the office the receptionist's still smiling so I give her a big smile back, after which I tell David Jones I'll let him know regarding the farm, decant myself from the realtor's, head for the nearest signal box, dial up the hospice and ask for Mr Kane.

No argument over the title this time and the hospital receptionist puts me straight through.

'Dr Kane here.'

I cut to the action.

'Does your husband keep anything of any significance at home?'

'Not that I know of. Why do you ask?'

I ignore the query and move onto the next question.

'When do you expect him back?'

'He told me seven-thirty. Why?'

'He always return when he says he will?'

'Always.'

'What about you?'

'What about me?'

'When will you be back?'

'Oh, quite late, actually, because I have to attend one of those interminable meetings to save the hospital. Why?'

Because I need to visit her home and take a look around, that's why.

Only I don't tell Sally Kane that.

People get funny if you tell them you're going to break into their domiciles.

Chapter 6

THE GUN IN THE LEFT-HAND DRAWER

Number 48 Daisy Drive, Dashiell, is Location, Location, Location, just like any respectable realtor's property ought to be. Not the worst house in the best street but you could call it unpretentious, if you didn't happen to be a real estate agent.

At 7.13 pm on a dusty Friday evening I find a white picket fence with a hedge next to it, a BEWARE OF THE DOG sign so burglars can be sure there isn't a dog to beware of, and a lawn as trim as David Jones's manners that looks like it's been treated with floricides, pesticides, fungicides, and artificial colouring.

There's a white-painted house to match the fence, a neat driveway ending in a garage to match the house, and a garden that could pass for a neatly-tended graveyard, no flowers by request.

As night closes in it feels like the house is the one doing the surveilling, the way a statue can look at you out of sightless eyes.

I unpack the Smith & Wesson, park it under the hedge in the company of the coat, and amble up the driveway whistling *Give My Regards to Broadway*, a difficult number due to all the jerky bits, like the last thing on my mind's a break-and-enter.

Correction, *home invasion*, because that's what they call it now, the same galahs that decided shoplifting's shop stealing, actresses actors, and geographical locations need to be stripped of their apostrophes, for reasons best known to their mothers.

I track the alarm wire, flick the switch and turn off the

power at the Main for good measure. I then smack the glass out of the back door with the butt-end of the torch from Vinnies and let myself into Chez Jones via the tradesmen's entrance, making sure I leave the hatchway wide open behind me.

The torch needs a good shake to make it function again, like a geezer experiencing problems with his prostate.

I make a detour to the bathroom where I unhook the glass from the porthole.

Then I start in on casing the joint.

There's an exercise bike in the middle of the living room floor and the torch gives up the ghost as the jewellery box from the master bedroom finds its way into one of my skyrockets, as a result of which I have to pick the lock to the study in the dark.

The study contains a chair, a desk and a lot of shadows.

I drag open the drapes.

At 7.23 pm, the desk's got nothing on it but a photograph in a gilt frame and several coats of lacquer.

There's just enough light to see the happy snap's a honeymoon shot and that Sally Kane looks just as good in a bikini as she should while David Jones looks like he wandered into the wrong photo parlour entirely. He's wearing a suit, but it's not of the variety you generally bathe in.

I use Mobile No. 9 to photograph the photograph before slotting it back on the lacquer and returning my attention to the desk.

By 7.27 pm, there's only time for one drawer so I choose the one on the left. I'm assuming Jones is right-handed and right-handed people keep items of consequence in their left-hand drawers, don't ask me why, I'm a gumshoe, not a shrink.

I step back, kick in the drawer, yank it open and Braille the contents.

Inventory:

A packet of paperclips.

The expected miscellany.

And the unexpected gun.

The gat's a Vickers Luger with a four-inch barrel capable of firing nine-millimetre parabellum and possessing a 32-round snail magazine, fully loaded and with the magazine release off, all dressed-up and nowhere to go, de rigueur for every real estate agent afraid for his life.

I know what to do so I do it.

At 7.29 pm and 30 seconds by the radioactive indices of my chronometer, I return the banger to its hidey-hole and do a final finger dance through the left-hand drawer. I come up with something I haven't noticed prior because it's all neatly tucked up amongst the drawer's lapped dovetails – a scrap of paper the size of a sheet of Cottontail extra-strength – just as a set of tyres crunch onto the driveway and a spray of light sprinkles its fairy dust through the window.

In the brief illumination I make out the words *Singing-teacher* and *Debtor to H. Stowe* and what looks like an address, but the light quickly fades to black and footsteps sound on the gravel so I pocket the papyrus, slam shut what's left of the drawer, smear a fingerprint-removing sleeve over the top of the desk, drag closed the drapes, bang shut the hatch, and kick-start my way back through the desirable domicile.

That's when I knock over the exercise bike and that's when the hoofbeats outside break into a canter.

Just as I reach the bathroom, I hear David Jones throw open the front door and swear when he discovers the light doesn't work. He comes in anyway because this is his goddamn home. The through-draft tells him the back hatch is open, which means the burglar just left and the back door must have been his escape route.

I hear him hurtle through the living room, crash over the exercise bike, swearing as he goes, before heading for the back door just like I meant him to – that's why I left it open.

I chuck the torch out the bathroom fenetre, obtain some sort of footing on the edge of the bathtub, heave myself up through the aperture, and get set to make my departure.

Only it doesn't work like that.

Nothing works like that.

I land on the torch and go into an ankle-roll and in the all-enveloping darkness sense something in front of me and that something is David Jones. David Jones is putting the question and he's not about to take No for an answer, except using my greater reach I don't give him a No, I give him a Maybe in the form of an aikido-palm to the acromion process of scapula, borrowing the full force of the forward momentum of his fist to deflect his vertebra prominens into the wall behind me and Jones into cloud-cuckoo land. I then sidestep, roll, turn, stand, steady and reorientate, before hoofing it back down the driveway, gathering the coat and the armoury from the hedgerow as I go and getting the hell away from 48 Daisy Drive.

When my mother held me in her arms on that fateful evening forty-five years previous she couldn't in a lifetime of drug-struck hallucinations have imagined her only son catching his breath on a side street in an Australian country town in the middle of nowhere with stolen goods in his possession and no visible means of support, on the lam following a home invasion, having knocked down a law-abiding citizen in the process, busy packing an equaliser into his shoulder holster.

Except for the country town bit, I doubt it.

But then, I never really knew my mother.

Maybe she could.

Maybe she did.

Maybe that's why she did it.

'You what!'

Sally Kane looks aghast.

It's still night and we're perched on a street corner in Dashiell and pedestrian traffic's flowing around us like we're sticks in a stream. I've just informed Sally Kane that I broke into her home and smacked her husband about a bit in the process.

She seems to want to hear it again so I tell it to her again and when I've finished, she says, 'But why did you do it?'

'To obtain information regarding which you weren't all that forthcoming, when asked.'

'Such as?'

'Such as anything.'

'And what did you find?'

I don't tell her about the gun. Tell her about the gun and she's going to get colder feet than the pair of iceblocks she's already wearing on the end of her beautiful pins.

'A piece of paper,' I say.

'And?'

'That piece of paper might provide the clue we need to help us solve the mystery of David Jones.' I throw her a glance. 'By the way, you didn't tell me he sang.'

She looks like she might have made a mistake hiring me.

'He doesn't.' She frowns. 'Look, what do I tell him about the – home invasion?'

I dig out the jewellery box.

'You don't tell him anything, because you don't know anything. Instead, when you get home, you tuck this jewellery box under the hedge. Then you go to your room like you probably always do and when you come out of your room you tell him, Why, David, it looks like that awful burglar must have helped himself to my jewellery box!'

I pass it across to her.

'That supplies a motive for the burglary and at the same time puts you in the clear.'

She contemplates the jewellery box.

It contains diamonds and sapphires and maybe a lot of memories.

'After which you go outside and conveniently discover the jewellery box under the hedge. End of story.'

Sally Kane shakes her beautiful head.

'But it's never the end of the story, is it, Mr Scutt?'

I tell her the same thing I tell Imogene, that all stories end pretty much where you want them to.

The answer doesn't satisfy Sally Kane.

'So, meanwhile, what will you do?'

'I'm taking myself back to Sydney where I'm going to pay a little visit to a singing teacher.'

Chapter 7

THE DOG IT WAS THAT DIED

When I was a kid, going to see singing teachers wasn't in the curriculum.

In fact, when I was a kid, being a kid wasn't in the curriculum.

Because when I was a kid – after my mother left and my father dumped me on Aunt Rube and Aunt Rube pulled me out of primary school because my classmates were bullying me pretty well on a daily basis – my aunt became my teacher.

And the curriculum Aunt Rube taught was detecting, which meant that I didn't learn things like the capital of Siam and what Genghis Khan got up to and how to control a scrimmage and the point of any of the Grimms Brothers fairytales. I learnt centre-of-life stuff like self-defence, ballet, languages, knots, firearms and anatomy, with a bit of piano thrown in for good measure.

Supplemented by a lot of stories about hard-boiled detectives.

As a result I've learnt to take nothing for granted in this world.

As I approach the singing teacher's, my mind's full of unresolved suspicions. Why would David Jones take singing lessons if he didn't sing, unless he was using the lessons as a front?

And if he was using the lessons as a front, why didn't he tell Sally Kane about them?

Because the way I figure it, our friend Jones at some stage possessed a slice of activity on the side, in which case fake singing lessons would make a lot of sense by way of an alibi while he's in the process of making covert visits to his concubine.

It's not much of a lead but it's the only lead I've got.

I continue up Hesketh towards Valentine's — the apostrophe's mine — the park on the left full of codgers and prams wheeled by teenagers and dogs defecating on the tulips. The sun's midday rays are ricocheting off my white fedora and back into the hole in the ozone layer, my white-sided shoes are carefully picking their way between the potholes on the trottoir and my eyes are checking out the oleanders for hidden marksmen, the codgers to see if they're packing equalisers, and passing traffic for vehicles driven by assassins intent on killing me.

The address turns out to be that of a joint desperately in need of a visit from a bulldozer.

I shove aside a bush full of thorns the size of scimitars to proceed via a set of well-worn steps to a verandah that contains a leaking gas meter, a wooden bench well past its use-by date and cluster-housing for an extended family of arachnids.

The doorbell doesn't work because there's no need for doorbells in a graveyard, so I employ the knuckles with nil result. I'm just fishing out the good old skeleton keys when I hear what sound like wounded hoofbeats — one foot down, one foot dragged, a pause, a tap as of a blind man's cane coming down hard on bare boards followed by a dull thud as the first foot comes into action again, and the sound of the drag once more.

When the door finally opens I feel a prickling at the back of my neck like someone's behind me. Before me I see nothing but the darkness of a deserted hallway until I make out a sparrow of a woman leaning on a walking stick, wearing an orange hairnet, a dress that's busy fading to shroud, and the sort of footwear that wouldn't look out of place on Mickey Mouse's squeeze, Minnie.

'Mrs Stowe?'

The figure frowns.

'My name is Alice Cantor and I wish you people would stop bothering me.'

Half of me is watching something moving behind her while the other half responds.

'I'm interested in singing lessons.'

'I don't give –'

I don't hear what she doesn't give on account of the shadow in the hall's taking shape and there's no time for much in the way of evasive action.

The thing spears for me and I drop to the ground under it, a snarling, screeching Inferno-dweller of a being with more teeth than a piranha, against which a karate chop would be no more than an exercise in futility, but I manage to get my hands around its throat and hold it away from me, at the same time as I'm squeezing the murderous life out of it.

But the dame's got into the action now, screaming like a Banshee, and she's got her walking stick up and she's flailing away at my head with its steel-encrusted handle and it won't be long before she breaks it – my head if not also the walking stick – so I figure it might be a step in the right direction to release my hold on piranha-fangs and focus instead on defending myself from the crone.

'Let go of Rocket, you horrible man!'

So I let go and the crone leaves off with the stick but only in order to pick up the death dealer which I now make out to be a small, off-colour, nondescript-looking cur with a head too big for its body and badly in need of a haircut that has suddenly fallen peaceful in the close embrace of its materfamilias while I wipe the gore off my snout with a nose-wipe.

'Look, lady, I'm real sorry about the –'

She's a shaker.

'Mister, I don't want to know what you're sorry about, just go!'

I figure that departing right now wouldn't be the sharpest step in the pas-de-deux.

'I just need a minute of your time, lady.'

She takes a squiz at me.

'Are you a policeman?'

She's already called me 'you people' and now she's followed it up with an inquiry regarding the possibility of my being a rozzer so I'm beginning to see a pattern here that I'd be well advised to attend to.

'Lady, if I was the fuzz I'd have plugged Fido by now.'

She glances at me.

There's intelligence in the eyes and I see them soften.

'I suppose you're right.'

'All I need is a few answers.'

The crone gives it a couple of beats, during which the shakes turns into a nod.

'All right, but don't go upsetting Rocket again.' She waves a claw towards a hall stand. 'You can deposit your hat there.'

I do like she says but before I track the form twisting its way down the hall I toss a final Captain Cook over my background.

The denizens of the park are still there, with the addition of a kookaburra laughing fit to duff itself, a dame in an off-green tracksuit is lumbering past the duck pond, and a bunch of schoolgirls is making their way past the house in a flurry of soft hats, innocent faces and scatology.

Old dames have old kitchens and Little Miss Twisty's is no exception.

There's a table and chairs, a rickety old sideboard and a couch.

But what I'm pondering while the crone's wrestling with the Lipton's is, Where's the pianola?

'You must excuse me,' she says as she sets a couple of cracked cups in cracked saucers on the table in an equally cracked voice, 'but I've got out of the habit of visitors since Harry went.'

I look away from where the pianola isn't and back at Miss Twisty.

She's got eyes like burnt cinders and knuckles with lumps all over them.

'Did you say Harry?'

She gives me a queer look.

'Yes.'

'Was it you or Harry that was the singing teacher?'

'Harry.'

'And what do you mean, "went"?'

The crone starts splashing out the tannin.

'I mean that my Harry – passed on.'

I figure it's too late to make with the condolences so I stay on song.

'And Harry would have been' – I consult the scrap of paper – 'Mr Stowe?'

The cinder-eyes contemplate me for a moment over the orange-flavoured tea cosy before looking away as she fumbles the rug over the teapot and parks herself in a chair.

'That means you're definitely not from the police, Mr –'

'Green,' I tell her. 'Peter Green. But why would it matter if I was from the police?'

She shrugs, or maybe it's just part of all the twitching.

'Because if you were, you'd find yourself on the other side of the door.' She takes a sip of the tea. 'But if you don't mind my saying so, Mr Brown, while I do accept you're not from the police, there's still something decidedly – how should I say – *different* about you.'

She contemplates me over the cup.

'Who are you, what are you and what do you want from me? And don't say singing lessons again because if you do I'll puke.'

'I –'

That's when the dog starts barking, a high-pitched, constant yapping. I figure it's because someone's outside and the pooch is just doing the job it's paid for but I've got the crone to this point and if I depart now I might never get her back to it. So I stay right where I am, perched on a stool at the rickety table sipping tea and asking questions, but by the time the dog's shut up and the crone's showing me the door all she's discovered is I'm inquisitive, and all I've discovered is:

Harry Stowe was a singing teacher;

Harry Stowe's pushing up daisies in Greenlawn;
Before attaining that status he taught David Jones singing;
All this occurred years ago.

The crone's handing me my chapeau and making with the felicities.

'Do you know Oliver Goldsmith, Mr Green?'

I can do blacksmiths but goldsmiths are a bit out of my league.

'Can't say I do.'

'Well you should. He was an eighteenth-century writer who wrote a lovely poem containing the line, "The dog it was that died".'

I look at the dog.

It's cradled in the old dame's arms, one eye in the shaggy head open and contemplating my nose.

'The townsfolk in the poem,' Little Miss Twisty says, 'were worried about the health of a man they believed to be beyond reproach. He'd been bitten by a mangy dog and they feared the bite might be fatal.'

She shifts her Minnie Mouse feet on the stoop.

'It turned out it was.'

She bends to put the dog gently back on the floor and with all the bending and twitching, plus the low voice, I have to strain to hear the punchline.

'Except that what happened was this man of impeccable character lived, and the dog it was that died.'

I nod but I haven't got the foggiest what the old dame's on about, unless it's that the barker that bit me might be going to cark it.

Chapter 8

INTERLUDE WITH AN EX-

It's late and public transport's missing presumed dead. As I make the approach to what in boat dwellers' circles passes for a front yard, there's a Black Hole of Calcutta where my coracle ought to be.

Dinghies are a live-on-board's lifeline.

You find your lifeline missing, you want to know why.

I select another dinghy from the forty or so on offer on the softly-lapping shore, launch it, remove my plates of meat from the whitesides, park myself in the driver's seat, fit the oars into the rowlocks, take the equaliser off Hold and put it on Maybe, and start rowing.

Twenty minutes later I come across my dinghy tied to the stern of the *Wooden No*. The shades are down and slivers of light sneak out into the harbour darkness around the edges.

I check about me.

The usual shipping, no unusual suspects.

I park the oars, clove-hitch the coracle to the stern next to mine, pick up the footwear and step sock-footed onto the swimming board.

Ferries are flat-bottomed and stable and the *Wooden No* is no exception.

Other tubs will list when a hundred-and-eighty-pound joker downloads himself onto it but not this baby.

I fist the gat, make my way to the hatchway and peer inside.

The interloper's back's towards me and he's leaning over the portside bench, a medium-height joker and slightly built, but it's the slightly-built jokers you got to watch in this world. They're the ones that have to defend themselves.

There's a good fathom between the two of us but I figure I can cover the distance using the bow thrusters. I park the hardware and am just preparing for take-off when the joker turns. The joker isn't a joker at all but a dame with a familiar face – but it's not a familiarity I want to carry further. This causes me to lose my balance on the launch pad, turning the fall into a tumble-turn, and I end up on my knees before Salina like I'm proposing to her all over again.

'Really, Rainbow!'

The dark roots are greying under the peroxide, the tall frame's on the gaunt side of svelte, and the expensive wardrobe's a mite worn, but the icy frigidity of Salina's being and the big, black, vacant-looking handbag on the table tell me I haven't made a mistake with the ID.

I get up off my knees fast.

'Where have you been?'

You'd think she was still my wife.

'Uh, seeing Sophie.'

'Who's Sophie?' She touches her hair as she makes the accusation. 'Another one of your floozies?'

I let the bouncer go through to the keeper, noting in the process that the wicket's in even more of a mess than usual – lockers open, drawers out, lids off jars, carpet torn away from the parquet – like she's been searching for the meaning of life even more desperately than usual.

'You've been through my stuff.'

'You should have been a detective.'

I find myself a vacant beer, operate the ring pull, take a swig to steady the peripherals and consider the situation.

Going by the number of empties, Salina has consumed four five-point-twos and is well into her fifth.

She always liked her lubricants, and that reminds me.

'How are . . .?'

'The kids?'

She frowns into her beer, remembers something and puts it into words.

'Imogene's fine,' her voice is chill as an iceberg, 'but I'd still prefer you stay away from Scarlet and Rhett. They're at a critical stage of their development and your visiting only disturbs them.'

The sea's coming up.

As is the request.

'I need more money.'

'I already paid you a year in advance' – I do the calculations – 'a couple of weeks ago.'

Facts don't cut much ice with Salina.

She's more an opinions person.

'I've spent it.'

It comes out *shpent*.

She uncrosses her eyes and slams down the can.

The boat rocks.

'Look, Rainbow, you wouldn't know, but bringing up kids is expensive.'

Then she goes for the big one.

'After all, they're *your* kids.'

She's not looking at me, like there's something stopping her.

I shrug.

It's only dough.

'Okay, I'll give you another grand.'

Her eyes harden.

Salina's strong on suspicion.

To her, Sophie's another woman and if I'm chucking her a big one without argument there's got to be a catch in it.

'Why?'

'You said you needed the money.'

Her face tells me she doesn't buy that and her words confirm it.

'There's got to be more to it than that.'

There is more to it than that only I've never been big in the bargaining department so I fish the dough out of my Y-fronts and am just handing it over when Salina pulls out her wallet, ripping it open so fast that something flies out and skitters across the chart table to me.

It's a happy snap.

In Wideascope, Wake-up-to-yourself and Technicolor.

Salina and Imogene.

And flanking them, a couple of medium-size but handsome brutes I might never have seen before, except that also I might have.

'That's not the twins.'

Salina looks uncertain.

You'd think she'd know her own children.

I reach for the snap.

'No!'

When people say No and also add an exclamation mark at the end of it there's got to be a reason and being in the line of work I'm in, naturally enough I'd like to know what it is.

I make to replace the moolah and that's when Salina removes her fist from the happy snap.

I check it out.

Salina and I have blue eyes.

So does Imogene, but the other two kids' peepers are brown.

Doesn't mean capsicums.

Blue eyes can throw brown.

Rube taught me that.

But Rube also taught me to look at the bigger picture.

So I look at the bigger picture and the bigger picture tells me that the twins in the happy snap are definitely not mine.

Chapter 9

GENES WILL OUT

I haven't clapped eyes on the twins since they were fat little maggots of ten.

After that there was no contact because Salina wouldn't allow it.

I was allowed to see Imogene but Salina didn't want the twins confused, disturbed or upset.

Then *she* didn't want to be confused, disturbed or upset.

Then she didn't want their uncle of the moment to be confused, disturbed or upset.

There was always a reason, even when there wasn't one.

When I last saw them, they were tallish, dark-haired and potato-faced and therefore could conceivably have been fathered by me.

But the kids in the chromatograph are short, blond and beautiful and therefore could only conceivably have been fathered by somebody else.

If teenagers are respecters of anything, it's genes.

It's just a suspicion.

But Salina confirms it.

'So now you know.'

That's the answer to one question.

Now for the second.

'When you suspected Tony –'

Her eyes are on the money.

So is her mind.

'Clint.'

That's the answer to the second question.

Clint was one of Salina's lovers.

He worked for Telstra, came to plug in our phone and ended up plugging Salina.

I always suspected there was more to it than that.

Now I know there was.

A set of twins more.

But I play it casual.

'Good old Clint still with the telecommunication shysters, then?'

Salina nods, like she suspects this isn't the question she's getting paid to answer, in which case she suspects right.

Now for the fourth question, the one she *is* getting paid to answer.

'When you first suspected Clint of cheating on you, how did you –?'

'Suss him out?'

It comes out *Shush*.

Tears spring to Salina's eyes and when she shrugs again it's with her orbs fixed on the last empty beer can. Her mouth is twitching, like the memory still hurts, like it all happened just the day before yesterday and it's my fault instead of anyone else's.

'In the way that every woman does.'

'Could you spell that out for me?'

I like having things spelt out for me.

Saves a lot of trouble when you look it up in the dictionary.

'I made friends with one of his fellow employees and persuaded him to get hold of Clint's telephone records.'

She goes to drain the can, remembers it's already drained and lets it slip out of her mitt to clatter onto the floor.

'And his phone records revealed text messages from hundreds of women, all of them wanting to be connected to Clint, or by him or with him or through him or whatever the preposition of the moment happens to be.'

She wipes the back of one hand across her eyes.

'Damn you, Rainbow!' She grabs back the photograph. 'Now, can I have my money and go?'

I chuck her the wad.

'Make sure you leave me my dinghy.'

Somehow it comes out sounding like *dignity*.

For a long while after Salina's gone I sit staring at the three-quarter moon, downing whiskies one after the other like they're water. I keep drinking long after the alcohol has ceased to do any good, long after the taste has stopped registering on my olfactories. The more I drink the emptier I feel of everything else.

The sight of Salina rowing off in the stolen coracle reminds me of the night she decided to pitch in her lot with Clint. Short, handsome, blond Clint lurking in our little, narrow-gutted home, waiting for the suitcases to be packed so he could lug them out to his station wagon – the wheels I'd helped him choose long before I knew he was boffing Salina – with plenty of room to stow my wife and her suitcases and the kids in. He refused to look in my direction as I sat on what had once been Salina's and my bed of roses but was now a bed of Procrustes, wishing him somewhere I had never wished anyone before, even after my one and only visit to Sunday school . . .

About midnight, I start the engine and cast off – much like Ulysses after the fall of Troy except that I've got no Penelope to make my way back to – in search of yet another mooring, the dinghy dragging in the *Wooden No*'s wake like a codicil to yet another memory I'm busy trying to erase from my cerebellum.

After three hours and another half-bottle of Glenfiddich, I find what I'm looking for in one of the thousands of little inlets the Sydney coastline provides for husbands hiding from ex-wives and criminals and creditors and the cops – plus anyone else that might happen along, much like Pandora. The bobbing red buoy has mussels and slime hanging off it and looks like it hasn't been attached to anything for years, much like an ex-husband. I boathook the sisal out of the sea, fumble the line through the hawsehole and belay it to the cleat up in the prow of the *Wooden No*.

I straighten the mattress that Salina looked under and

didn't put back right, listen to the groan of the bilge pump as it gets on with the Sisyphean task of keeping the *Wooden No* afloat, and fall asleep dreaming of Sally Kane and her beautiful peepers and the way they'll look when I finally tell her, Yeah, your husband's got a paramour but I'm available, with a love for Yours Truly that's deep, grateful, everlasting and impossible to ignore.

Or at least chuck another couple of grand my way so I can pay a bit more to my ex.

Chapter 10

FROM HERE TO PATERNITY

The Bell Telephone jokers aren't playing ball.

First up, they can't categorise me.

You're either an account-owing, an account-paying or a complainant, and if you're none of the above you're little better than a waste of potentially lucrative soundwaves.

I eventually score a humanoid, who says he's in this world for no reason other than to assist me. I know I'm asking for trouble but there's no other way.

'I need to talk to Clint Eastwood.'

Parents have a lot to answer for and that includes Clint's – Mr and Mrs Eastwood – and it's a while before the humanoid's able to reply, and even then he's still laughing fit to blow his connection.

'As in *The Man with No Name* in *A Fistful of Dollars*?'

I give him three beats to work it out of his system.

'Go ahead, punk,' he tells me, 'make my day.'

When I figure he's had enough time to get over it, I steer him back to rationality.

'He used to be in Sales.'

The humorist dredges his memory for another homily.

'Don't go away now!'

The recorded music tells me that Someone Just Called To Say They Love Me, which is more than the queue snaking out from the telephone booth does. By the time the father of two of my children makes an appearance on the other end of the telecommunications system, they're ready to turn-turtle me.

'Hi, mate!' Good old Clint, everybody's amigo. 'Who did you say it was again?'

I tell him who it was again and there's a series of clicks as Clint makes the connection.

'Mate,' he says at last.

Clint should be a chess master.

Then he could have all the mates he wants.

As it is, he has to settle for people who hate him and their husbands.

'I need a favour.'

'Anything, mate,' he says in a rush, 'you just got to ask.'

So I ask.

Not the hard question, at least not straight up, just the easy one, so as not to scare him back to where he came from.

'I need the boat swept.'

'Someone bugging you?'

You could say that.

Then again you could say a lot more.

Only I don't do either.

Instead, I tell him where the boat is and then make my way out past the hostile-eyed crowd.

First things first and the first thing is to meet up with Clint.

At which point I can get him to do the second thing.

My expectations are that good old Clint will be unchanged and that he'll arrive in a Telco van with advertisements all over the sides. But when he screeches to a stop at Leatherjacket Inlet at the far end of Yellowtail Park, it's in a red whizz-bang firecracker with smoke billowing out of its oesophagus and a fortune in effluent pouring out its bowels. He steps out onto terra firma and looks just like Santa Claus – bald head under a red cap bearing the words KEEP IN TOUCH! in silver foil, comfortable belly, cute little beard, everything bar the little red uniform, the belt and the free patooties.

'Mate,' he tells me.

'Mate,' I tell him back.

His eyes veer to the broken-down wharf where I've parked the *Wooden No.*

'This the boat?'

No, I want to tell him, this is a seaplane, heavily disguised, with its wings removed and its pontoons ripped off and yet somehow still afloat in the water.

But irony's a luxury I can't afford so I content myself with a simple affirmative, along with the rider that I need it checked out for listening devices.

It doesn't need a sweep but I don't tell him that.

He puts a hand on the *Wooden No.*

It's the same hand he put on Salina.

'I also require the Telefunken records of a real estate agent.'

'Of actual conversations?'

I shake my head.

'Of actual phone numbers – callers and called.'

Clint takes his hand off the boat, scrabbles a nose-wipe out of his Santa Claus outfit and uses it to towel the hand with which he's caressed Salina. He then replaces the nose-wipe, goes into doubtful mode and responds to the request.

'Look, I don't know about this, mate.'

'I don't know about an action for paternity, either.'

He takes off his cap and scratches his head as if that might be the way to better understanding, like praying to God or believing in the Australian legal system, of what constitutes the complicated social labyrinth of debt and obligation, in this world or in any other.

'Mate, you know as well as I do that accessing phone records is against the law.'

'So is living on a boat, but I'm doing it.'

'What if I get caught?'

'I've already caught you.'

He shuffles the cap back on his skull and because it's wrinkled it now reads OUCH!

He breathes like it hurts.

'All right. Give me the number and name of the subscriber.'

I haul out the card that Jones dealt me and give Clint the name and number of the subscriber. He keys it into a little machine that relieves people of the risk of writer's cramp or of having to use what might pass for a brain.

'That's not the department store, right?'

I ignore the riposte.

'How long will it take?'

'This sort of information's not just lying around waiting to be harvested, you know, it's all highly confidential. And if I get caught –'

'It's a question, not a debate and the question is simple: How long will it take?'

'It will take a while,' he says, 'before I'll be able to come up with anything and even then there's no guarantee it will be what you want, mate.'

So I remind Clint again what he's done and what I might do about it if he doesn't do it and he says, Mate, I'll try, but that's the best I can promise you, mate.

To which I tell him, Mate, you'd better do better than that.

Chapter 11

LITTLE MISS TWISTY REMEMBERS

I don't recognise the voice coming out of the Telefunken, in spite of the fact that it's using one of my monikers.

'Mr Grey?'

The voice is high-pitched and tremulous.

'Who's asking?'

The voice tells me who's asking but I don't recognise the name.

'The lady with the dog.'

Why didn't she say so in the first place?

'What can I do you for?'

'I've just remembered something.'

'Don't say anything over the phone. I'll come to you.'

'Can you come immediately?'

The dame sounds impatient, like if I'm too long she might forget what she's remembered, might even forget she had anything to remember, might even forget she's forgotten.

Normal detectives possess their own conveyance.

Only I'm not a normal detective.

Accordingly, I take the omnibus to Bondi Junction, underground-it back to the city, catch a cab to Camperdown and make with Shanks's pony down the home straight to the crone's joint. By the time I'm being meeted and greeted I might be in a lather of sweat but at least I haven't brought company.

'You took your time, young man.'

She's wearing a dress with purple diagonals against an orange background, too much rouge and an anxious expression on her dial-up.

'What I've remembered is –'

'Let's take the dog for a walk,' I interrupt, 'and you can tell me en route.'

The dame shakes her head.

'Rocket's never been for a walk in his life. He's an agoraphobe.'

'We'll take a walk without him, then.'

We park the pooch and I get the dame down the steps and across the road to the park.

'Do you remember, Mr Blue, my inquiring if you were from the police?'

'Yeah.'

'Well, the reason for my inquiry was that when Harriet died the police thought I'd done it.'

'Don't you mean Harry?'

'Harriet was Harry. Harry was a woman. We were lovers, Harriet and I.'

That's how she knew I wasn't from the cops.

The cops knew Harry was a woman while I didn't have a clue. I don't like not having a clue.

'What did you and Harriet being lovers have to do with the fuzz?'

We reach the lake and turn.

'Once they discover you're lesbian,' she tells me, 'you become fair game.

Despite all their talk of non-discrimination, if you're lesbian the police think you're guilty of all the sins of the world, short of creating the hole in the ozone layer, and they even keep their files open on that.'

I already know this because Aunt Rube has spent her lifetime in a similar situation.

'Second, Harriet died of an overdose of the painkillers I was taking for my rheumatics.'

She pauses.

'And third, because the police found traces of the painkillers in my system – why shouldn't they, for God's sake, I'm a cripple – they assumed that Harriet's death was the result of a suicide pact gone wrong.'

'Whereas,' I say, 'in reality, Harriet did herself in.'

The old dame shakes her head.

'Young man, Harry simply isn't – I'm sorry, wasn't – the suicidal type.'

'You think Harriet was murdered?'

'Mr Green or Brown or Grey or Blue or whatever your name is, I don't think Harriet was murdered, I know she was. The only thing I don't know is who did it. Or who would want to kill her for that matter.'

'Do you remember anything else?'

Miss Twisty frowns.

'Someone paid us a visit while I was pegging out the washing and that same person found my pills and forced them down poor Harriet's throat. Dear little Rocket was a witness to the deed.'

The dame staggers, pauses and rights herself before pointing her feet in the intended direction once more.

'Rocket barked the house down' – there are tears in her eyes – 'and I didn't do anything about it. Instead I just kept pegging out the washing.'

She shudders.

'When I came back inside – I recall it was just after midday – there lay poor Harriet, the love of my life, the empty pill container beside her, dead.'

'How come you're suddenly remembering all this now?'

She shrugs.

At least I think it's a shrug.

It's hard to tell with all the twitching.

'I haven't just remembered it, it's because I want to help you, Mr Brown.' She wipes her eyes with the sleeve of the dress with the orange background. 'I know what you're trying to do because you haven't once mentioned this niece of yours, the one who was so anxious to take singing lessons. Plus all your questions are about Harry.'

It's my turn to shrug.

'So what does that prove?'

She glances at me then quickly glances away and down at the ground because there are potholes in it and it's taking all her strength just to stay upright.

'It proves, Mr Green, that you're a private detective.' She takes a deep, shuddering breath. 'And that you just might discover who murdered my Harriet and afford me some finality in the matter.'

One thing the old dame hasn't remembered is to bring her house key, meaning I've got to enter through the side window. I then brave the acrid smell of an old dame's domicile, the dog smooching up like we're old friends and open the door. The crone taps her way straight past and on up the hall: she's racked with pain from her rheumatics and all she wants now is to lie down with Rocket on the couch in the kitchen. I pat the pooch on its funny big head before getting myself back up the hall and out the door.

Chapter 12

THE HARD CELL

The jail's a jail and there are two ways of getting into it.

One's by committing a felony.

The other's by taking a bus.

I take the bus.

Two things I don't like about jails.

One is you mightn't get out again.

The other is they take your shoes.

Every time I fight them over the footwear and every time I lose.

'So what's with the shoes?'

The screw chucks the two-tones in a bin, along with the belt, the wallet, the keys, the mobile, the bus money, the fedora and most of what's left of my self-respect.

'It's the rules, pal' – the screw's not taking any prisoners – 'and if you're worried about the restrictions to your freedom of movement, go see a chiropractor.'

Rube's seated with her hands on the prison-issue table, the shadows of bars lacing a rough noughts-and-crosses fretwork over her prison greens. She's ready with her favourite line from one of the talkies she used to screen on the dining room wall, the same line she greeted me with when my dad dumped me on her all those years ago.

'Here's looking at you, kid.'

I shrug.

I'm a big boy now.

It doesn't cut any gorgonzola with Rube.

'How they treating you, Rube?'

She moves her head but the fretwork stays where it is.

'Like you'd expect them to treat any criminal.'

'Only you're not a criminal.'

It's Rube's turn to shrug.

'Everyone's a criminal, it's just a matter of whether you get caught or not.'

'Look, I've got this case . . .'

Aunt Rube climbs down off her stool, ambles away from the bars, then turns and contemplates me.

'Who'd a thought,' her voice is a murmur, 'my little boy a Dee.' She shakes her head. 'I remember the day my brother dumped you.'

She's got this faraway look in her eyes.

'He was driving a Kombi painted all the colours of the – well, you know – and he had this blonde arrangement perched next to him wearing a set of boobs that could have been missiles set for take-off and he had an impatient look on his kisser like he had the world to save, his only problem being you.

You were spat out of that van like poo from a pig's bum on steroids.'

It's not a simile I'd use but Aunt Rube's Aunt Rube.

'He didn't even say goodbye. Your mother's body still warm and him with a new moll and here he is getting rid of his kid and he doesn't even get out of the van to do it.'

She shakes her head.

'Rube, he tells me, look after the brat, would you, there's a good girl.

Always called me a good girl, Albert did, even though I was anything but.

And that's the last I see of my dear brother, not just for a while but for always, leaving me with a traumatised orphan to look after.' She throws up her hands like she's surrendering. 'For God's sake what would I know about bringing up orphans!'

'You did okay,' I tell her.

Her laugh is hollow at the best of times but this isn't the best of times, and the laugh comes out hollower than ever.

'Okay? Okay? Here's me, a private detective that looks

like Mata Hari, reads old-time detective stories and watches nothing but movies featuring Humphrey Bogart and Edward G. Robinson and James Cagney, her head way back in the beginning of the last century, for God's sake, and her heart in crime, in charge of a kid who's in trauma.'

Again the laugh.

'You poor little bugger. What chance did you have? A name like Mr Rainbow – which I made you keep because I decided it would be character building.'

She shakes her head.

'Okay, tell me what you need.'

I frown at her.

'I got this situation, see, namely a joker with no paperwork.'

Aunt Rube nods.

'What else you got?'

'I got his prints.'

'And now you want to see if he's got form.'

Everyone who's ever been in the nick has fingerprints and every set of prints comes complete with a name.

I tell her yes but also to hurry.

Because through the bars I can see a screw heading our way, which makes it a fair bet that the interview's over.

'Get in touch with Rory,' Aunt Rube tells me. 'Rory the Terminator. He knows all about you. But watch him. He can be a mite on the edgy side.'

Rube's just got time to add an address before the guard breaks up the party.

There's a new sadist at the door, and she advises me that the shoes will have to be destroyed.

'You don't just destroy shoes!'

The guard smirks.

She knows where it hurts.

'When we decide they're a threat to security we do, pal.'

She wants me to argue because that's when they can call in the support and when they call in the support is also when they're allowed to hurt you.

I see them shovelling Aunt Rube along the barred corridor back to her cell and the screws that are doing the shovelling aren't wearing kid gloves or any sort of gloves unless they're the ones with horseshoes in them, so I go quietly.

One, because I've got nothing on my feet to make a noise with.

But, and far more important, two, because I don't want to make things any harder on Rube than they already are.

Shoes are a dime a dozen.

But you can't buy yourself a new aunt.

Chapter 13

THE HIT MAN

The address Rube gave me is a prefabricated lean-to at the wrong end of the worst street on the crook side of the railway line in a burg at the bad end of the planet.

I'm not carrying a shooter because you don't visit jails wearing concealed and unlicensed weaponry unless you wish to become a permanent resident of the jail yourself. This makes me feel very naked and feeling very naked raises my anxiety level up around the danger mark.

I pick my way past an acre of dog droppings and a bunch of burnt-out jalopies to a falling down gate guarding a cracked concrete pathway leading to a door with an axe sticking out of it, at about the height you'd normally expect to find a door handle.

A buzzer sounds but no one answers my rataplan so I open the hatch by way of the axe handle and make my way along a hallway littered with empty whisky jars. The place in better times might have gone by the cognomen 'kitchen' but now is no more than a graveyard for cockroaches and a repository for the detritus of rats.

That's when I'm jumped.

I end up flat on my extended vertebrae with a little one-legged joker standing over me, head craning down on a too-thin neck, carving knife in one hand and a crutch in the other and intent on his face to kill me.

Rube did warn me Rory's a mite on the touchy side.

Also that he's a black belt in karate.

'Who are you?'

Well, he knows who I am because at some point in my

existence Rube would have supplied a description. Only he hasn't put one and one together, so I figure I'd better help with the addition, because I don't want to die due to faulty paperwork.

'The name's Rainbow.'

I scramble to my hoofs and fetch my hat off the floor and replace it.

'What sort of name's Rainbow?'

I've heard it before and I'll hear it again.

'Rube told me to look you up.'

The one-legged joker's eyes soften in much the same way rock turns to molten magma during a volcanic eruption.

'So you're Rainbow?' He says it like nothing out of the ordinary's just occurred. 'How is old Rube these days? Still giving everyone a hard time?'

I inform him that in fact she's doing time.

'What did they nab her for?'

'They wanted to screw someone and they asked her to help with their inquiries but she wouldn't play ball so they framed her.'

Rory nods like it's just another game on the pinball machine and the little chrome spheres are bouncing pretty much like they always do.

'She want to be sprung?'

I tell him Rube might well want to be released from prison but that isn't the purpose of my visit. He asks me the purpose of my visit and I tell him and only then does he lower the cutter and only then does he start to relax a little.

I can see it takes a lot to relax Rory.

He's not a relaxed kind of guy.

'Who's the mark?'

I tell him who the mark is, checking the assassin out as I do so.

He's something under middle height and possesses the aforementioned thin neck. He's wearing words on his T-shirt that would have rendered him jailable even before they invented political correctness, and one leg of his crumpled trousers is pinned up over the vacant jamb. He looks like nothing more than the one-legged killer he is, but I remind myself he comes complete with a reference from Rube.

'So why do you need the check?'

'Request from the wife.'

'Any complications?'

'He could have a doxy on the side.'

'Anything else?'

'He doesn't exist.'

Rory nods.

He knows about people not existing.

In fact he's a specialist in people not existing.

'How can I help?'

'You can tell me if he's been through the sieve.'

I've obtained a copy of David Jones's prints from his business card using grey powder – the usual mix of chalk, mercury and powdered graphite – which I then took a happy snap of and this is what I hand Rory.

He scrunches it into a pocket without looking at it.

'I'll see what I can do.'

A figure appears in the doorway.

'Everything all right, boss?'

The lunk's so big he could double as a wardrobe.

'Took ya time to get here.'

The giant's tone turns to petulance.

'I warned you he was coming, didn't I?'

'And you reckon that's enough? Just rolling over in bed and pressing a button? For a start I didn't know who it was and for a finish all I had time for was to grab a knife and get myself behind the door.'

The lunk's whine turns into an even bigger whine.

'I was involved, wasn't I, boss?'

'Well it's time you got yourself uninvolved.'

Rube put me onto Rory as the best man for the job.

I remember the way he greeted me and now I see how he sends the big man packing and I understand why Rube put me onto him.

Rube knows I don't like hurting people.

Rory, on the other hand, kills for a living or lives for a

killing, however you want to play it, and however you want to play it, Rory would have to be one handy little potato to have on your side.

Apart from which he clearly doesn't take No or Maybe for an answer.

'Is that all?'

'I might need you to do a bit of baby-sitting.'

'No killing?'

'None.'

Rory parks the disappointment.

'So who's the Mind?'

'It's a real baby,' I tell him, 'my daughter Imogene. It's worth a dee.'

'Five Cs!'

I'm running out of moolah but this case is starting to get a spread on it so five hundred's where the money pegs out as far as Rory's concerned.

'It's for Rube.'

Everyone owes Rube and Rory would be no exception.

He scratches an armpit, cocks an eyebrow, tugs at a lug, sniffs and eases his crotch.

Rory's an ease-his-crotch kind of guy.

'I need my head examined,' he says finally, 'but I'll do it.'

He grabs the crutch – the one with the big-bore barrelling in it, plus the sights and the breech and the triggering mechanism and all the rest of the accoutrements that go to make up an assassin's rifle – swings himself across the kitchen and deposits the knife in the sink.

In the backyard I make out a dog chewing on a bone.

It's a big bone, the size and shape of a human femur. It's still got plenty of gristle on it, and while the dog's a big dog, it's got its work cut out just gnawing on it.

I note the axe has been removed from the door and the lunk's chopping wood with it, like he's trying to get something out of his system. There's fat ballooning out of the armholes of his faded-blue singlet, and his pectorals are bulging. But just like I haven't asked about the dog or the bone, I don't inquire about the axeman, either.

According to Rube, Rory's always worked in mysterious ways, his wonders to perform.

Besides, the foot pinchers from Vinnies are killing me.

Chapter 14

THE MAN WHO HATED BEETHOVEN

Dashiell's turning bleak as I make my way from the station clutching my fedora. A wind whips about my ears at butcher-freezer temperature while a joker clings to a ladder hanging a sign over the main drag bearing a picture of a clown, together with a warning that Fate's heading for Dashiell, watch this space.

The wind drops for a moment and so does the sign, making it read 'Fete' not 'Fate', but tell that to my synapses.

When Sally Kane rang I was grubbing dry rot out of the hatchway and Panic was at Sally Kane's elbow.

'I can't go on,' she says. 'Tell me what I owe you and we'll call it a day.'

I wasn't in the mood to call it a day, a week, a year, or a month of Sundays, so I stare at the passing shipping and tell myself, None of us can go on, but we do, because it's what makes the world go round, from water birth to marriage, divorce to death, and funeral parlour to the wide blue verandah.

'What's the problem?'

'Can I speak over the phone?'

That's what phones are for, specifically.

'Shoot.'

'It's just that I – I think David knows.'

'Knows what?'

'Knows that I'm – that you're – Oh, I don't know . . . All right, that we're checking up on him.'

'What makes you think that?'

'He saw you at the house. He knows what you are, if not exactly who you are. I showed him the jewellery box but he wasn't convinced. He knows he's being watched and I know he suspects that I have something to do with it.'

'Thinking isn't knowing, people's minds –'

Sally Kane cuts across me.

'I happen to know about people's minds, Mr Scutt. I'm a neurosurgeon, remember?'

'I'll be there tomorrow.'

As per usual, Sally Kane has selected the trysting place and this time it's the hillside just around the corner from the farm with the solar panels on it. It's the same hillside overlooking the cottage I first noticed when Jones showed me the farm. The new shoes I got from the gentleman outfitters' slip while I'm climbing, the parcel I obtained is heavy under my armpit, and although I'm on time, it's another half an hour before I pick Sally Kane up on my radar, moving up along the ridge in a roundabout sort of way.

'I hope you haven't been waiting long,' she says on arrival. 'I've been at yet another of those meetings to save the hospital.'

Sally Kane's hair is glistening in the sunlight, her long dress wrapped around a pair of pins Mitzi Gaynor would have been proud of.

She throws herself down and while she's catching her breath I busy myself looking elsewhere – at the cottage, the sheep mooching around the cottage and, perched in the foreground, my new palominos with the dirt of the road still upon them.

I dust them off.

'I'm sorry, but I've changed my mind yet again, Mr Scutt. I think I – just wanted to see if you were – committed. Now I simply want to get to the bottom of this or I'll regret it for the rest of my life.'

She's agitated for about the length of a Baby Browning but collects herself, takes a swig of fresh air and finds herself ready to speak again.

'There is another matter, as it happens.'

'What might that be?'

She looks at her hands.

'I know it sounds silly, but David hates a particular piece of music. It's Beethoven's Ninth. Do you know Beethoven's Ninth, Mr Scutt?'

Rube always kept me abreast of the classics, so I'm able to tell her Yeah.

'Well, David came home one evening while I had it playing – the Naxos one with Nicolaus Esterházy conducting – and he simply hit the roof. He was so angry that he grabbed the CD player and hurled it out the window. And the window wasn't even open.'

'Sounds like he doesn't like it, all right.'

She looks worried.

'So what do we do now?'

'We put it all in the mix.' I give it two beats, like a thought has just entered my brain. 'You ever get to town?'

'I have a neurosurgeons' conference next week. Why do you ask?'

'Because by then I should have something for you.' I take a deep breath and the breath's got Sally Kane's perfume in it. 'I'd like you to make a reservation for the conference. Only you won't be attending, because we'll be taking a boat ride instead. Meanwhile, first thing tomorrow I'll pay another visit to your husband.'

I look down the hill towards the house.

The sheep have been joined by a shepherd.

They'll be safe now.

At least until they're trucked off to the abattoir.

Chapter 15

THE CASE OF THE RECYCLED RECEPTIONIST

First thing tomorrow it's cold and I'm hunched against the prevailing iciness behind a variegated pittosporum across the road from 48 Daisy Drive. I'm using the magnifiers to scan the frost blanketing the lawn which is just starting to thaw as David Jones – wearing a light-tan attaché case and a fixed expression – steps out of the front doorway and onto the porch. A dribble from the overhang splashes onto the left shoulder of his well-pressed suit causing him to flick a glance skywards. He checks out the sightlines to the left and the right of him before making his way along the seamless concrete pathway to the white-painted front gate. He lets himself out onto the footpath, looking back at the house like he's checking for something more than just rising damp and then both ways again as he clicks the gate shut behind him. He tucks the grip under his arm, turns right and picks his way with neat, precise steps towards town.

I follow, but at a discreet distance.

I'm garbed in the second set of gear the gentlemen's outfitter provided me with – vide licit, a brace of foot-pinching laughing-sides, white moleskin trousers, open neck shirt, oversize tweed jacket to accommodate the Smith & Wesson 645 in the shoulder holster, a pair of Zeiss binoculars crammed into a side pocket, the whole affair topped off with a curly-brimmed Akubra.

Accordingly I appear pretty much like any other denizen of Dashiell and therefore unlikely to excite much attention.

Jones doesn't spot the tail, even when my new boots upend me on the icy tar macadam outside the hot bread shop. (What do you do if you slip on ice when you're tailing someone? Rube would ask. Freeze, I'd tell her. Good boy! she'd reply, and I'd get the vodka.) He still doesn't see me, despite shooting a baker's-dozen worth of glances over his shoulder, like he's got a specific Nemesis in mind.

Beneath all the Circus and Fate signs as Jones steps into the caffeine den I note the unfamiliar girl stepping into the offices of Jones, Jones and Jones, the Realtors You Can Trust, just past the nice white Holden on the sun-favoured side of the carriageway.

Trust your feelings, Rube told me, on account of feelings is what distinguishes humans from automatons.

So I trust my feelings and my feelings tell me this must be the other woman.

It's not the receptionist I met, anyway.

Description: late teens, just the age to suit a mid-life-crisis male, even one married to someone as beautiful as Sally Kane, big goggly glasses, barber-tousled hair, neat black dress, everything shipshape and yet somehow something frazzled about her.

Like she just got out of bed and the bed had more than just her in it.

I'm still looking as Jones emerges from the caffeine parlour, brown Thermo-cup held away from his body so there's no chance of its contents soiling his bag of fruit, briefcase held just so out on the other wing, hailing and greeting passers-by like any good dream-flogger. He pauses at the bureau doors before entering to look at the For Sale signs. He seems alert and ready, but for all that like some sort of delicate sea creature, the sort that slips innocently through murky waters, hurting nobody, until something very nasty turns up and it finds itself dead.

The sort of thought that occurs to someone in love with another man's wife, desiring to discover hope where there is none, who assures himself, Yeah, someone's going to duff the poor bastard, it's only a matter of time, and when that happens I'll be available for a free consolation.

Bad thoughts, thoughts of which Rube wouldn't approve.

After ten minuets, Frazzle doesn't emerge but David Jones does. He climbs into the Commodore in the company of a young couple with moonbeams in their eyes and drives in the direction of out-of-town.

I wait until the car's gone before I cross the road, walk the block, surveill the sidewalk, de-walk the block, then enter the offices of Jones, Jones and Jones, the Realtors You Can Trust. Miss Frazzle is behind the reception desk.

'I'd like to purchase some property.'

Her eyes have trouble focusing, like she's just walked out of a cinema screening a movie in three dimensions and she's forgotten to remove her glasses.

'They didn't tell me anything about Sales.'

Blinking myopically, she peers at the pretty pictures in the window, like the answer might be there.

'I'm sorry but Mr Jones isn't in at the moment.'

She looks at the paperweight on the desk before casting her peepers back to me.

'There is one listing that's both, however. Mr Jones told me about it. Rent it or sell it, he said, it doesn't matter which.'

She pauses and considers me.

'Would you be interested in that, perhaps?'

I know that voice from somewhere.

'They've been trying to get rid of the place, oh, for simply ages, although maybe I shouldn't tell you that, you being a potential purchaser, so to speak, and also it's solar-powered, which is another pain in the butt because when there's no sun there's no power.'

She shoots me a gaze with a lot of vagueness in it.

'I'm new in real estate,' she tells me in case I hadn't guessed it, 'so I'm not altogether –'

She doesn't have to tell me what she isn't altogether because I've recognised the voice.

It's the receptionist from the hospital.

Miss Frazzle's been recycled.

'Mr Jones has already shown me that joint.'

'Oh.' She scrabbles among her papers. 'Well, if you could just tell me what your name is . . .'

I tell her what my name isn't and turn to go before stopping again, like I've just been slapped in the face with a flounder.

'By the way, what happened to the other receptionist, the happy one, the one with the gay demeanour?'

'Um, she was' – Miss Frazzle searches for the appropriate euphemism, can't find one, so settles for the truth instead – 'sacked.'

'Why?'

'She changed the ringtone on Mr Jones's mobile.'

Just like Imogene did to one of mine.

I'm still smiling, only now I've got teeth.

'She wouldn't have changed it to Beethoven's Ninth, by any chance, would she?'

Frazzle's eyebrows appear above her goggles.

'Goodness, how did you know that?'

The sentence ends in the air.

Only this time the rising inflection's justified.

Chapter 16

SETTING THE CATS RUNNING

'Edith Burton?'

Good old Clint came up with the name after he'd romanced some dame several beaks above him in the Telco pecking order. The name stands out from a long list on the realtor's chat-lines because it's a regular contact, once a month, smack on the dot, reliable as the tide, and potentially just as relevant in the scheme of things.

'I understand you're a friend of David Jones.'

While there's no response from the other end of the Alexander Graham Bell, at least there's no hang-up either, no Bugger off and stop bothering me, so for the third time in this one-sided dialogue I drop my dulcet tones into the dropjaw.

'I have reason to believe there have been threats to David Jones's life.'

'Since when did department stores have lives?'

The usual joke but delivered in lead-weighted, drawly, deliberate Chicago tones.

No hint of anxiety, just the obvious witticism, like Edith Burton's had it all ready for a rainy day and doesn't need to look out the window to know there's a storm coming.

Then the follow-through.

'Who are you?'

Funny name time, to suit the joke.

'Mr Magenta,' I tell her, 'but friends call me Pinky.'

'Well, Mr Magenta, or whatever your name is, I hope you know what you're talking about, because I sure as hell don't.'

The records show that it's going to be another two weeks before Jones gets back in touch with his lover. That means two weeks of uncertainty, two weeks during which Edith Burton will berate herself for not paying more attention to this man with the obvious cryptonym, two weeks of barely endurable suspense, a fortnight strung out on those things they stretch sails on, also known as tenterhooks.

I suspect friend Burton's not the type to wait for the world to come to her – she's much more likely to get out into it and help herself.

The teeth of autumn are bared for their first nip at the winter cherry and par consequence I'm wearing a black sailor's cap and red sailor's windcheater over blue-jeans with a slight tear to the right upper-sleeve of the jacket into which I've inserted the micro-cam. I'm perched on the port side of the park bench with my arms folded in order to get the lens facing the right way and repelling all boarders while a pair of ankle biters squabble over a shovel in a sandpit, the leaves still on the trees because this is Australia, the natives are evergreen and everything in the garden's lovely.

Until something happens and it isn't.

'Mr Magenta?'

Edith Burton's out of the same mould as David Jones, someone who, on the Gemini principle, he could conceivably be attracted to. She's got a hint of Spanish olive to her but is neat as a pin, of middle height, with brown eyes and close-cropped hair. Her avocado-coloured parka is open at the front with the hood down, and underneath she's wearing a white T-shirt, joggers, close-fitting jeans with the zip at the front – which on women constitutes a design flaw, in my opinion.

'Just look at those kids,' I say, slick as oil. 'Now why is that spade so important to them?'

But Edith Burton isn't buying what I'm selling.

Finger on the button I click her frowning.

Snap of the competition to show Sally Kane.

'Look Mr Joke Name, let's forget the kids, shall we?' It might be cold but Edith Burton's got the gloves off. 'After you phoned I nearly called the police.'

I glance around.

A couple of jokers are taking in the autumn air and a gaggle of schoolboys are playing hooky from the reformatory, but there's not the barest whisper of the siege men, the boys in blue with the flame-throwers and the capsicum, so I bring my peepers back to lover-girl.

There's no threat of a concealed weapon – knife, toy gun, knitting needle, so forth – only you never know with illicit lovers, they're not always all that predictable.

She hunches her shoulders and spreads her fingers, the way dames can do these days, like they've put in more than the odd evening on the tae-kwon-do mat and they're dead keen to share the benefits of their training.

'So why didn't you?' I ask her.

She doesn't tell me why didn't she.

Instead, she makes with her own series of question marks.

'Call it curiosity.' She cracks her knuckles. 'But first I'd like to know what this Jones person could possibly have to do with me. Second, I'd like to know why it should concern you. And third' – she pats a side door of her avocado-coloured parka – 'I'd like to know why I shouldn't call the cops after all.'

I'm over the niceties.

'The answer to your fourth question, stated or otherwise, is that someone's out to get David Jones.'

It's a Mexican stand-off, without the wave.

I can't tell her that Sally Kane's hired me because she'd inform Jones of that fact.

And Burton can't admit to being Jones's lover because I could tell anybody.

'On the off chance I'm at all interested in what you're trying to sell me, Mr Spray paint, how do you know someone's out to get this person?'

'Let's just say I've got evidence.'

'And what might that evidence be?'

I stretch the truth and come up with another cliché.

'I have reason to believe that Mr Jones's life's in danger.'

I'm watching her closely but for all her reactions I could have told her that David Jones had turned Mormon.

'And what's your role in all this, Mr –?'

I glance at the kids then back at Burton.

'Let's just say I'm an interested observer.'

Burton hasn't shifted position.

She's still tense and she's still ready to launch into a flying fandango.

'So why bother me?'

I wait until my pulse steadies.

'Because I believe you might have a personal interest in the welfare of David Jones.'

Edith Burton has turned away and is watching the kids. I figure she thinks I am, too, only I'm not, because I'm watching her.

And because I'm watching her and she thinks I'm not, I see her stiffen, the slightest of backward jerks of the head. I snap a shot of that and several more unhappy shots as she gets up off the park bench and hurries away. She takes small neat strides with her elbows close to her sides and speeds up as she disappears through a gap in the randomly planted evergreens on this cool autumn day with the kids held apart and spitting at each other from the safety of their respective mothers' arms, the spade abandoned on the ground between them.

I've put Edith Burton on the alert, which isn't a bad thing if you want to set the cats running.

And setting the cats running is precisely what I want to do. The object of this exercise isn't to discover the identity of David Jones's lover but to find out who Jones is and why someone like Burton might be worried if his life's in danger. I can only do that by spurring her into some sort of action that might be described as untoward.

Chapter 17

THE DESIGN FLAW

Ask me the precise moment I'm certain I'm being followed and I'd say it's when the omnibus drops me at the junction of Druitt and George, up alongside the Rathaus.

No one tailed me to the park, I'm sure of that.

I'm also certain I'm Omo-clean when I board the omnibus, there being no evidence of anything apart from a feeling.

And in this game, as Rube says, while instinct's fine, feelings don't butter parsnips, nor promise you anything but a lie-down role in a final farewell at a funeral parlour.

Several more punters get on – a blond kid clutching a scooter, a sum of accountants and an old dame lugging a green tartan granny cart – while only one joker boards the bus behind us.

I get off at Wynyard and take the third 412 that happens along, parking myself next to a geezer who looks like he ought to be on life-support instead of a bus. I plan to alight at the edifice named after our late and unlamented Queen Victoria.

I turn to help the codger whose hand is as thin as a coathanger, skin as dry as landfall after six months at sea and as cold as the polar ice cap. One hoof trembles on the running-board while the other waves about in the air like an antenna. I reach out to stop him tumbling into the gutter.

That's when I look back and that's when I see Edith Burton, only this time it's without the benefit of an appointment.

She's fourth out of the bus behind ours and if I hadn't been busy helping Herb – Herb's the name, just call me Herb, everyone does, even the dog – I wouldn't have noticed her.

When I last saw her she was wearing an avocado-coloured

parka with the hood down. Now, the parka's black and the hood's up, and if she's got brown hair, you wouldn't know it. For the record, I only know it's her because of the way she moves: like a wildcat in the jungle with its claws sheathed.

I could call seeing her again a coincidence, only I don't call anything a coincidence.

Accordingly, I believe she's following me.

But I want to do more than believe, I need to know it for a fact.

Knowing things for a fact is what keeps sailors alive, knowing for a fact that all the cleats are in place, the rigging's secure, the steering cable's not hanging by a thread, there isn't a crack in the hull, and the bilge pump's fully operational.

It's also what keeps gumshoes out of the graveyard.

I set Herbie down, even more frail-looking now he finds himself at street level, and we have a little chat about the weather.

We both hope it will hold.

That's when I make my move.

In seven-tenths of a second I've completed the instep swivel-spin on the metatarsals and am clattering over the mosaics decorating the floor of the Queen Victoria Building, heading for York.

At Market I chuck a right, followed by a left into George – not to the ship circus in Darling Harbour but towards the Semi-Circular Quay. I then slow to five knots, anchoring long enough to glance in a shop window and nod at the mannequins wearing their post-summer finery. I tack sharply back into Wynyard, secreting the sailor's cap under the shirt while I'm in the Gents', but not the jacket, due to the fact the Smith & Wesson needs it for cover. I stop to buy a newspaper at the kiosk under the destination board, take the escalators back to York, then make the final preamble along the straight to the boat show, much in the manner of a middle-aged joker that's losing it.

And in all the glancing at reflections, doublings-back, stoppings and glancings between my knees, there's no sign of Edith Burton, in black parka or avocado-coloured turnaround or crimson top or no parka at all – no sign of her face, no sign of her walk, no sense of her presence, no glimmer of anything to do with the actual or soi-disant lover of David Jones at all.

Until I get to the boat show.

And then I spot her again, but only because I run into a fellow boater who's also wearing a red sailing jacket with blue jeans. After I palm him the newspaper and we separate, Edith Burton exhibits one of those dead giveaway nanoseconds of hesitation that can afflict even the most experienced of surveillers – she must decide which of us to follow.

She's stripped down to white T-shirt, jeans, and sneakers – the chameleon has turned into a sailor – but she's still Edith Burton and I still recognise her.

There are a number of ways of losing a tail.

First – Aunt Rube's Regola Numero Uno – don't let them know that you know that they're tailing you.

Well, it's too late for that, my friend, Edith Burton already knows that I know.

But it's not too late to apply the second rule, which goes something like this: be patient or be dead.

It's a truth, universally unacknowledged, that a surveiller has to eat, drink, sleep and go to the lavatory, just like any other micturating creature on this planet. This is why the well-trained surveiller always carries food and drink, plus something to pee in.

But that's only when they know they're going to be surveilling.

And that's something Burton couldn't possibly have known and therefore couldn't possibly have been prepared for.

I pay a visit to the toilet, in order to plant the concept 'toilet' in her mind.

Then I make for the marina where there are no toilets, just the heads on boats whose use by the general public is verboten.

After that, I saunter off to lunch, settling down at a table and tossing a serviette over my knees and ordering up big like I haven't eaten for a week and am getting prepared for a slap-up.

Five minutes.

Ten.

I see Burton haul alongside portside-aft and linger near the Damen und Herren.

The waiter passes into posterity.

I raise my wine glass and note in it the reflection of Edith Burton, secure in her delusion that I'm engaged in nothing more than anticipating my repast, while she's glancing longingly at the sign that says Damen und Herren.

Seconds later, she ducks into the Damen.

That's when I make my move.

You can't be followed into a kitchen, not without creating a serious disturbance.

One person might get away with it but in your average industrial-strength kitchen, two more's a crowd.

There's a chance that Edith Burton's still in the Ladies' but an even bigger chance she's done a hit and run and the bigger chance has won because I can hear her slamming the door open and following this joker she's only just had the pleasure of meeting. The big, awkward-looking affair has stuffed the gat down his jeans and chucked the jacket onto the gas burners and is now clutching his cap. He lopes past the pots, pans, sous chefs, bottle washers and waiters' assistants, the overseas students with garbage bins and mops in their hands and the future in their hearts and astonishment in their eyes, and out through the back door. He then belts across the promenade and clatters up the steps and into a carriage of the monorail just as the doors close.

I can see Darling Harbour laid out below me like a painting by Brueghel, a painting with too many people in it and all of them too much the same, until the carriage is halfway around the first bend and there she is, standing by a palm tree in the forecourt doing a 360-degree turn, slowly, deliberately, surely quartering the environs. As she does this, the fly on her jeans is open, exposing pink underwear, because a front-loading zip on women's jeans is a design flaw, and for Edith Burton, when she realised I was doing a runner, it was first things first, and the first thing was to relocate me. When she'd done that, or given up, whichever came first, then and only then would Ms Burton, professional follower, attend to the adjustment of her clothing.

Chapter 18

BACK IN THE SLAMMER

I present myself in the slammer wearing the purple-and-white pintos that got nailed in the last case but one – a slug through the portside aileron from a Remington Rolling Block 1871 – and it's icy like a morgue in winter. Me and Rube are in the south-wing visiting-cell, and Rube's in the sort of mood that makes me feel like a kid that's got caught stealing from the gift box on charity day at the poorhouse.

'Rory's just been to see me.' She's hunched and is staring out through the bars. 'He says he's fed up with all the killing.'

When Aunt Rube hauled me out of Baisson Primary and started in on my home schooling, I discovered that her idea of education was screening James Cagney movies on the cracked dining room wall, or handing me a book by George Harmon Coxe or W. R. Burnett or Hammett or Chandler, and dispensing her own particular brand of philosophy.

Along the way, I learnt the principles of logic, surveillance, self-defence, anatomy, pharmacology, body mechanics, several languages, ballet, and how to play piano.

I also learnt ethics.

'I told him killing's not on the agenda, Rube.'

Aunt Rube nods.

'But he's got a minder.'

'Who, Rory?'

'No, David Jones.'

I tell Rube about Burton – how she's in regular contact with the husband of the client, doesn't give anything away, and knows how to follow people.

'Prisoners on bail require minders.'

Rube's mind works like a computer, only faster.

'People can still have private lives.'

'That would make it a coincidence, Rube, and I don't believe in coincidence.'

Once upon a time that would have scored me a shot of vodka.

'I believe I taught you that, too, Rainbow.' Rube's silent for a moment. 'Tell me more about the minder.'

So I tell Rube more about Edith Burton and all the time I'm watching the screws prowling about us like dingoes around unattended babies.

'She could be anybody,' she says at last. 'ASIO, ASIS, CIS, DEA – any one of a number of acronyms.' She glances at me. 'That's words made up of initials, in case you don't remember.'

It's then that the door's knocked down or – the jail-place equivalent – the gate clangs open, and two screws – it's becoming a habit – charge into the room. While Rube's dragged kicking and screaming back to solitary by one of them, I'm advised by the other to get the hell out, visiting hours are over.

'What about the footwear?' I ask, leaving.

'Just piss off.' Which is jail speak for Goodbye.

I'm busy pondering Rube's take on Burton when Mobile C rings, its dial tone the theme from *Apocalypse Now*.

I dig it out of the portside aileron.

'That you, Rainbow?'

I've told Rory not to name names on the cellophane but I'm fast discovering Rory's not all that big in the listening department.

'No,' I advise him.

'Yeah, it is. Look, Rainbow, I got to see you.'

It's like Rory's brains have taken a powder along with the leg.

I hang up fast. Then I hotfoot it to O'Leary's. O'Leary's is doing a trade only it's not roaring. There's the odd piss-boy, a couple of travellers and a druggie in the midst of a delusion.

Rory's arrived before me and he's hunched over an ale with his eyes popping all over the place, even checking out Hank, the barman, and Hank's been here since Adam was a girl.

'Hi, Hank.'

'Hi, Rainbow, how they hanging?'

Hank pretends he's as butch as the next joker, hair poking out of the top of his pink singlet and muscles on muscles, when I know for a fact he shaves his shoulders.

I chuck him a frown.

He shrugs.

'It's just an expression, Rainbow.'

Hank gets over his agitation by rubbing hard at the top of the bar with what look like an unwashed pair of pink underpants.

'What's your poison today, Rainbow?'

'Same as it was yesterday and the day before that and the day before that.'

'That would be soda water.'

'That's exactly what it would be.'

'With . . .?'

'With carbon dioxide and a dash of potassium bicarbonate.'

I turn to Rory.

His face bears a hunted expression.

Rube warned me of his latest hang-up.

'Look, Roarer,' I tell him, 'if it's bullets you're afraid of, you might be in the wrong profession. But seeing you're in it, you can forget about being afraid, and tell me what you discovered.'

Rory shrugs.

'I put the prints in the system. I got this little mate, see . . .'

'Spare me the details. How long will it take?'

'What, the story?'

'No, the processing.'

'It's not a formal thing.' He shrugs again. 'Accordingly, it will take as long as it takes. Meantime, I'm staking out the kid like you told me to but it's giving me the creeps, because someone –'

I take a swig of the eau de nothing.

'Look, Roarer, you're a killer. Killers can handle killers.'

'Except I'm not all that crazy about killing any more, Rain, apart from which, this dame –'

That would be Burton, Madam Professional Burton, who would have done her own fingerprint check on me – courtesy of the Darling Harbour wineglass – and come up with Rainbow and via Rainbow she's come up with Imogene and having come up with Imogene she's also stumbled across Rory, so accordingly she's lurking with intent to discover what we're about, only I don't tell Rory that, the less Rory knows about things the better.

'Forget the dame and keep your eye on the kid.'

'I still don't like it, Rainbow.'

'You're not paid to like it.'

After Rory's gone, his eyes still darting about like a rabbit's at a summertime shoot, I linger a while with Hank.

'I need some advice, Hank.'

'Do you want that straight, too?'

I let the witticism pass.

'When you got out of the slammer after doing time for whatever you did time for – spare me the details – were you by any chance allocated a parole officer?'

Hank nods.

'We had to be in regular telephone contact.'

'How often? Daily, weekly, monthly?'

'Daily.'

'How long ago was that?'

He squeezes out the underpants in the sink.

'Years back, in the dark ages. Now they just stick a bug on you.'

Chapter 19

A DISTURBANCE
IN THE NIGHT

The moon's on the wane but it's still as big as Cyclops's eyeball, rolling across the open hatch of the *Wooden No*'s aft cabin like the orb of the giant in *The Odyssey* as he tried to duck the poker that Ulysses was trying to jam into his one eye, preparatory to making good his escape.

The wind's shifting, from north-east to east.

The *Wooden No*'s on yet another borrowed mooring, a hempen line attached to a two-ton block of concrete on the ocean floor all that's stopping the drunken tub from smashing itself to smithereens on the rocks.

The moonlight reveals a crumpled doona and a pile of dirty clothes while the boat dweller's trusty jam jar and an empty bottle of Johnny Walker Red clatter this way and that across the marzipan like a couple of dice in a crap game.

Coupled with these sleep-inducing phenomena, the boat's crepitating, the fairy fingers of Fate tapping away at the superstructure like it's trying to decide whether to sink me now, or allow me a few more moments of uncertain existence before curtain time.

To top it off, one of the mobiles rings, the one containing the theme music from *Dr Zhivago*.

I scrabble it out.

'Mr Scutt?'

A dame's voice.

Play it again.

'Mr Brown?' This time I recognise the dulcets. 'I do hope I didn't wake you.'

'It's okay,' I say, 'I wasn't asleep. What is it?'

'I've just remembered something.'

There's a series of clicks like Miss Twisty's bones are cracking. I hear the sound of the dog snuffling about in the background.

'Shoot.'

'What did you say?'

'Forget what I said and just tell me what you remember.'

For three rolls of the boat all that comes out of the cellophane is shuffle-shuffle-shuffle, click-click-click, the clatter of teaspoon against cup, an old woman's memory playing ducks and drakes with the facts and then:

'Oh, yes, that's right, two things, maybe neither of them important, but I had to tell you or I wouldn't be able to sleep tonight.'

Make that two of us.

'First – Are you still there, Mr Green?'

'Affirmative.'

'What? Oh, you mean, Yes. Well, first of all –'

She goes silent again so I make with the prompt.

'Yeah?'

The clicks go into overdrive but after a bit she comes back online.

'First, you believed that Harry was male and that told me conclusively you weren't from the police because the police . . . Anyway, we sorted all that out. But second, you thought that Harry was a singing teacher.'

An old woman's midnight ramblings – of course Harriet was a singing teacher, didn't the receipt read: Harry Stowe, Singing teacher, Dr to David Jones, et cetera, et cetera and so forth?

'Yeah.' I think about it, then I don't think about it. 'Because that's what she was, wasn't she?'

'Yes, Mr Brown, she was. But she also taught voice.'

My mind comes into focus.

'Meaning?'

'Meaning, Mr Grey, that Harriet not only taught people how to sing she also taught them how to speak.'

Extract from interview with Sally Kane:
'How's he talk?'
'I told you. Nothing.'
'I meant his voice.'
'Oh, David has what I would call perfect intonation.'
I re-enter the present, during which time Little Miss Twisty is still busy explaining.
'Come again?'
Miss Twisty comes again.
'I was talking about Harry's students. There were children needing help after operations to correct problems like cleft palates, adults getting used to dentures, accident victims learning to talk again, people needing to change the way they speak . . .'
The click of teaspoon-on-cup metamorphoses into something else, a code that might be making no sense at all, but is still trying to tell me something.
'What sort of people need to change the way they speak, Miss Cantor?'
A sigh or it could be the wind.
'Persons who want to get on in this world, Mr Brown. Whatever people say, Australia is far from being a classless country and the wrong accent can be like a police barrier at a crime scene – yes, Mr White, I do read detective novels – and can seriously hold people back from somewhere they'd rather be.'
I absorb that little homily, at the same time as I'm leading Little Miss Twisty on to the next stage.
'There was something else.'
'What?'
'The second thing you remembered.'
'Oh, yes . . . Well, the series of lessons had just been completed when . . .'
Click-click-click-click-click.
'What's that?'
But the dog's started barking.
I picture Miss Twisty gripping onto a chair as she talks, eyes dulling as she winces with the pain, her joints cracking

and the little dog – the dandie Dinmont or the agoraphobe or whatever it calls itself – prancing about and barking its crazy head off, at nothing more than the wind.

'Rocket, do be quiet! What on earth's the matter with you?' Then back to me. 'I'm sorry, Mr Black, what did you say?'

I tell her what I said but it's too late.

The barking has stopped, the clicks have ceased, Little Miss Twisty's voice has been cut off, the line's dead, and when I ring back all I get is the sort of signal that says the phone's engaged, you're wasting your time, call back tomorrow. After a while I give up, in case the reason the phone's engaged is that Little Miss Twisty's busy trying to call.

I'm still waiting when the arms of Lethe claim me and I'm still waiting again when I wake next morning, late, due to the disturbance in the night.

And I'm still waiting now.

Because Little Miss Twisty never rang me – or anyone else for that matter – ever again.

Chapter 20

DEATH AT NOON

There are chores to do on a boat in order to stop it sinking – the bilge pump to mend, re-pitching the hole in the hull that's reopened, and making with the bail out – so it's close to noon when I finally climb down into the coracle and close to an hour later when I step off the omnibus a couple of stops short of Miss Twisty's. I alight at the crossroads where the 437 chucks a right in order to make its circuitous way past the homes of politicians' grandmothers, then cross the park we traversed not all that long ago, moving this way and that in order to expose anyone that might be tailing me, but all the time heading in the general direction of Little Miss Twisty's.

I see no one.

That doesn't mean crabmeat.

Nor is there any traffic.

That's not unusual, either, except that there should be.

Not even the odd bus approaches along the carriageway. I can't figure the reason for this until I swing around the clump of trees at the southern end of the park and see the bus – just the one bus – and there's nothing odd about that either except for the mess of cops that's surrounding it, and the sort of barrier that Little Miss Twisty mentioned, that cops like to put up around crime scenes.

Six squad cars are spread across the road, red and blue fantasy lights flashing, twenty or so interested spectators craning for a glimpse of blood from the other side of the blue-and-white tape where they've been herded, an ambulance nosing its way towards the focal point, just to the fore of the bus.

I get nervous packing a gat around the fuzz.

They got X-ray vision for concealed weaponry.

I'm wearing the big jacket but am aware of the bulk of the S&W pressing against my ribs so I doff the trilby and park it over the equaliser. I realise I might appear to be paying my respects to whoever might require my paying my respects to, of which there might be a great need, or not much, depending upon your viewpoint in the matter.

That's when I see her.

Little Miss Twisty has never been straighter, a small, thin twig lying three-quarters of the way across the carriageway, arms by her sides, closed eyes facing heavenwards, so she might be asleep except for the marks on her face and the pool of what might be oil, but isn't, which has darkened a patch of her hair at the same time as it's matted it and which also appears to have glued the back of Little Miss Twisty's head to the tar macadam.

The marks on her face are consistent with her having been hit by a bus.

Or . . .

Three paces from the figure on the ground, someone in joggers is opening his heart to the rozzers.

From where I'm standing there's no way of hearing what he's saying so I work my way past the ambos with their stretcher and the gawkers, making especially sure to give a wide berth to the cop with the Sigourney Weaver face, until I'm near the back of the joker that's doing all the spraying and able to tune into the broadcast.

'She was going that fast. One minute there was nothing, the next . . .'

I miss what follows next, but then, 'Like a flash she was, like she'd been shot out of a cannon.'

Like she'd been shot out of a cannon?

Little Miss Twisty?

Miss Twisty could hardly manage a walk.

As I back away the cop's saying, But how do you account for the marks on her face?

No one seems to be paying any attention as I let myself

in through the rusty gate and up the steps and onto the dark verandah under the laughing kookaburra etched in the fanlight and in through the still-open front door from where whoever-it-was hurled the body of Little Miss Twisty after what must have been many hours of doing a lot of hurt to her. I move along the darkened click-click-click floor of the hall and into the kitchen where the wall clock reads just after one in the post-meridiem. The pooch is cringing under the sideboard, just his funny little nose and glinty little eyes sticking out, staring up at me like I might be yet another person or persons unknown come to do him or his mistress further harm.

'Come on, boy.'

Or girl or thing or whatever you happen to be.

I bend down.

'Good dog!'

There's blood on Rocket's head but the wound doesn't appear to be fatal and he doesn't bite my hand or even attempt to, even when I pick him up, falling immobile in my arms like a child's toy, even when I accidentally knock his head against the window frame in my haste to get out, because there are footsteps and voices screaming Stop! as I exit and belt up the main drag as fast as I can in order to distance myself from the knot of interested spectators around Rocket's mistress's body. I take a left up a lane, the sound of my pursuers fading until eventually all I can hear is the clatter of my palominos on the sidewalk, the shuddering breathing of Rocket in my arms, and the myriad interrogatories echoing in my skull regarding the passing of Little Miss Twisty.

Like: Why?

And: Why just now?

Meanwhile, I've got a dog on my hands.

I call Rory.

'How are you doing with the surveill?'

'Apart from the dame that keeps making the guest appearances, good as gold.'

'Can you look after a dog?'

'What, kill one?'

He sounds appalled.

'No, look after one, as in care for it, feed, kennel it, that kind of thing.'

He tells me, Yeah, because it so happens the palooka just bumped his off and he's looking for a replacement – for the dog, not the palooka – so I find a cab driver that takes dogs and get him to take Rocket to Rory, after which I keep my date with Sally Kane.

Chapter 21

THE BLACK CABRIOLET

Keep dames at arm's length, Aunt Rube always told me, they can be bigger killers than the Thompson M1928 trench broom as employed by Al Capone's boys when they massacred seven of Bugs Moran's heavies in a Chicago garage on Saint Valentine's Day, February fourteenth, nineteen hundred and twenty-nine.

But Sally Kane isn't at arm's length: she's seated in the beam of the dinghy, pressing her hat into her nestful of beautiful curls with one slender hand and clutching the bulwark with the other. The wind's freshening as I haul on the oars that are carrying us into ever deeper waters, the only movement around us – apart from the rowing – a dozen bird-limed yachts abandoned on their moorings, the ripples on the surface of the harbour, and a bunch of seagulls tormenting a shiny black seal a fistful of fathoms to windward.

I keep reminding myself that the reason for the boat ride is not so much to get Sally Kane alone as to discover the raison-d'être for Edith Burton, given the Burton dame's a mite too handy in the tracking department to be nothing more than David Jones's extra-marital squeeze.

I get us to a beach and Sally Kane perches herself on a rock overlooking the water.

I've told her about the phone calls and also about Edith Burton and she's looked at the happy snaps but she still says she doesn't know the dame from Solvol.

'Do you think they're . . .?'

'Negative.'

'But why else would he be making regular calls to her, if she weren't, if they weren't –?'

'That's what I'm asking you.'

'Perhaps –'

'Perhaps what?'

'Perhaps . . . I don't know, perhaps they're – related. Didn't you tell me they're alike?'

'Yeah.'

'Well, then . . .?'

I look at the seal.

'Aren't they a protected species, seals?'

'What's protection got to do with the price of salmon?'

'Just a thought,' she says.

After the seal's gone plus the birds and all the romance that wasn't and we've piled back into the coracle and I've rowed us back to where we came from, I realise I know what that seal's got to do with the price of salmon. I've known all along, if only I could admit it.

A black, nineteen-twenties two-seater people-mover in the shape of an upright coffin with flat-foot running boards, oaken-spoke wheels and damask curtains to the windows tends to stand out in a crowd, which means that whoever's at the wheel isn't worried about being in possession of a profile. A dozen corpses laid cranium to metatarsal is about the distance the car's staying behind me. I've just seen Sally Kane onto her train, and the black car's keeping perfect pace as I foot it along the boulevard. Its forward progress – in the vicinity of five knots per honorarium – leads me to suspect that it's not just employed for transport – it's also a tail.

Chapter 22

RETURN OF THE AXEMAN

It's close to midday when Rory's voice filters through on dead-man's mobile No. 17.

'I'm outside the kid's place and there's something funny going on.'

'Shoot.'

'You know the dame I was telling you about?'

'Olive skin? Tall for a dame?'

'That's the one.

Well, she's closing in on me and I want to know if I'm supposed to duff her, because –'

'No,' I tell him, 'I know who it is and she's only a minder, not a killer.'

'You could have fooled me.'

'Okay, rendezvous you-know-where in ten.'

'But it can't wait, Rainbow, I –'

'It's got to wait, pal,' I tell him, 'all of six hundred seconds it's got to wait.'

Rory's not you-know-anywhere when I get to O'Leary's.

I'm wearing the zebra-striped jacket and the new orange trilby I purchased from Serafino's to replace the fedora. While I'm hitting the sodawater I keep the head down because I'm not in the mood for socialising.

This isn't New York, it's not the nineteen-twenties

and there's no Eighteenth Amendment prohibiting the manufacture, sale and transportation of intoxicating liquor, but that's just for the blatts.

It doesn't mean Sydney doesn't possess joints like O'Leary's.

It just means you don't hear about them.

'You waiting for Rory?'

It's the palooka, the one that just bumped off Rory's dog, the one with the axe.

The joker's an ape, and that's no compliment to primates.

He'd weigh in at about the two-hundred-and-eighty mark and there's a long, suspicious-looking bulge under his non-matching tracksuit.

Never trust a joker in a non-matching tracksuit.

'I got a message for Rainbow.'

Rory's just sacked this watermelon.

Accordingly, there are two ways he could know I'm waiting for Rory, and at least one of them carries ramifications that aren't all that pleasant to contemplate.

'What's it to me?'

Uncertainty flickers across the pug's face.

'Ain't you Rainbow?'

'If I'm a rainbow you're a moonbeam and if you're a moonbeam –'

The nice thing about O'Leary's is that when there's a contretemps, the clients tend to ignore it and continue indulging in their drug of choice while the matter's resolved.

So when I accompany the ape outside and Hank's busy clearing away the broken glass, the upturned stool, the blood and the axe, nobody looks up.

'What's the message, Sunshine?'

'Rory says he doesn't need to see you. The message he gave me is: Everything's good.'

'Who sent you?'

'Rory did.'

I convince him that Rory didn't, a discussion that involves smashing his jaw.

'So who was it?'

'A voice,' he manages through the jaw.

'You always do what the voices tell you?'

'This one I do.'

'Who was it?'

'I don't know.'

'You work for someone you don't know?'

He manages a shrug. 'They pay.'

Why would someone pay someone to tell me everything's good when Rory himself has just informed me that it isn't?

That's the first question.

The second question is, Where's Rory?

The answer to both is pretty much one and the same and suddenly I'm several street numbers down the road from the speakeasy, my palominos pounding the pavement, my breath coming in the sort of rasps that could spring Aunt Rube from solitary, the new trilby gripped in my hand, and fear clawing at my heart for Imogene.

Chapter 23

THE KILLING ON CASTANET CLOSE

It's a long time since I've been to Number 21 Castanet Close but I'm familiar with the address because this is where I send the major portion of my ill-gotten gains. Rory's across the road where he's meant to be, slumped in the driver's seat of the wide-bodied pink Caddie he uses when he wants to travel incognito, a miniature Colt pistol dangling from the rear-vision looking glass, and a little star decorating the driver's-side wind-up. He's got the sort of look on his face he'd reserve for moments of absolute calm, like when he's about to kill somebody. Only he's not about to kill somebody, because somebody beat him to it and killed him first.

I don't waste time on the autopsy. My first reaction is to charge into Number 21 Castanet Close, gun blazing. But my second is to stay alive, so I prostrate myself by the coupe and shoot a couple of Captain Cooks along the *camino real* prior to focusing on the narrow-necked brick-veneer lean-to with the pink geranium in the cracked pot out the front where in another life I used to reside, directly across the carriageway from the Caddie.

Imogene's room's the one on the right. The silhouette of the fairy I made for her hangs in the window under the half-drawn blind. The moving part of the fenetre halfway up the box frame reveals a Chinese lantern with witches etched on it and a part-open wardrobe with a child's drawing of a three-legged cat Bear-taped to the sliding door.

There's the shadow of a movement at about the point where

the window turns into a sill.

Castanet Close is a wide street, wider still when there's a corpse in the car behind you, an even-money bet there's a second in the house in front of you, and the very real possibility the killer's still in the frame, all set to make it a trifecta.

The .45 is cocked but still in the cross-over under the jacket as I make my way – arms out, fingers spread, like Cagney in *Yankee Doodle Dandy* – to the front gate, at the slightest provocation ready to do the quick-draw, side-step and flip-roll onto the asphalt.

The side path's still got a slope to it like the Wall of Death at the Royal Easter Show, leaving enough room under the back of the house for Imogene to play hide 'n' seek in when she feels the need. The bell's still busted and the side door's still made of papier-mâché, so it's hardly a challenge kicking the hatch down. I whip out the Smith & Wesson as I stay on the stoop, right where I was when I kicked the door down.

Tripodi, Imogene's three-legged cat, has been lying in the hallway with a bullet hole through his brain long enough to attract flies, long enough to make clear he's never going to lurch about on his three legs again, but not long enough for the blood to complete its inexorable process of coagulation.

A sound comes from the direction of Imogene's bedchamber.

I dive over the dead moggie and into the sleepy-hole, Smith & Wesson at the ready.

Nothing.

No kid, no perpetrator, just a breeze through the open window with the fairy swinging in it, a Donald Duck clock on the green cupboard next to the bed telling me it's thirteen minuets after twelve, and too many memories – Imogene sleeping, Imogene unwrapping Christmas presents, Imogene . . .

I park the gat, tear the wardrobe door off its plastic slippery-slide, and yank Imogene's bed away from the wall.

Still nothing.

There's no blood in Imogene's room, I keep telling myself as I reupholster the gat and get myself in quick-time across to the window – there's no, repeat no, blood in Imogene's room.

The blind's hanging crooked, the fairy's still swaying at the end of its tether and there are marks consistent with footwear decorating the sill. But a quick shooftee tells me that apart from the Caddie on the other side of the carriageway, the street's still wearing the Vacant sign.

I stand with blistering eyes in the middle of Imogene's crumpled clothes, her books, her plastic macramé and her teddy dogs, trying to recreate in my mind what might have occurred a quarter of an hour prior.

The book on the unmade bed is *Where The Wild Things Are*, open at a page with a drawing of a monster with dirty big teeth in it, enhanced after publication, distribution and sale with scribbles of purple and blue crayon.

She always liked – make that *likes* – being scared, Imogene.

There's a real likelihood they got her.

They?

I don't know any They, only that Imogene's not here, and the street's deserted.

There's no blood in Imogene's room, I repeat to myself, nothing happened, or at least nothing that can't be fixed with an ice-cream.

I sense something behind me.

I spin around.

That's when I see Imogene, Imogene showing the effects of too many ice-creams, Imogene with an expression on her face halfway between laughing and crying, Imogene with dirt on her Levi's that can only have come from under the house, the place where I taught her to play hide 'n' seek in whenever there were people around that she needed to get away from.

I take a long breath, and I take it slow and easy.

'You all right, Immo?'

Imogene nods.

She's a small figure, shoeless in the middle of the hallway under the coat rack.

'What happened?'

'They hurt Tripodi.'

I cast an eye over the kid.

There are no marks on her, apart from the scars that must be all over her pysche, and the dirt.

'Who's they?'

I wait.

You don't push a kid, especially one that's just escaped something nasty.

She takes a deep breath, just like I taught her to.

'Mummy got a phone call and then she went away.'

I nod at the grey Telefunken that's parked among the detritus on the table at the far end of the hall.

'That phone?'

Imogene nods.

I cross to it, pick up the receiver, whack the necessary buttons, and the phone advises anyone that cares to know that the last call was from a private number, which therefore cannot be revealed.

I replace the receiver and turn back to Imogene.

'What happened after Mummy went away?'

Imogene manages to steady herself.

'I heard them climb in through Mummy's window and I knew it wasn't Mummy because Mummy's got a key so I took off my shoes and I ran out the back door and down the back steps and under the house and hid just like you taught me to and there was lots and lots of noise and I knew they were hurting Trippie and Trippie doesn't like being hurt so he made lots of noise and I wanted to go and help him but I knew I mustn't because you taught me not to so I squashed really hard against the water eater and then everything went quiet, and after that I heard your footprints so I came out.'

All in one breath.

I nod.

'Clever girl. Now you said "they". Can you tell me how many bad men there were, Immo? Think careful. You heard my footprints. Did you hear theirs, too?'

Imogene thinks careful but after thinking careful she can only shake her head, the tears brimming as she stares at the matted furball that used to be her cat, lying not all that far from the neat little row of bullet-holes drilled into the architrave.

'I tried to, Daddy, but Trippie was making too much noise for me to count them.'

There's no time for any more cross-exam.

I can hear Salina hurrying down the path. She's not going to be all that delighted about the wardrobe door being ripped out and lying on the carpet in Imogene's room. Nor the blood on the floor of the hall and the front hatch hanging off its hinges. Nor the guilt she's going to feel for leaving Imogene alone in the house to keep a rendezvous with someone that doesn't exist. That guilt's going to be converted into anger at yours truly so accordingly I shove the still-warm corpse of the moggie under my jacket and turn to face the mother, just as she makes her appearance in the hatchway.

Go on the offensive.

I can do offensive.

'You got to go into hiding,' I tell her.

Salina looks from the bulge under my jacket to Imogene then back to the bulge under my jacket.

She looks terrible weary all of a sudden.

'The usual place?'

I nod.

'The usual place.'

She sighs.

'The usual way?'

'The usual way. A cab hailed in the street – no phone bookings – not the first one, and one that's travelling in the opposite direction to the one you'll be going in. After you've ridden around for a while, get out, go through the shopping centre or whatever there is to go through and when you come out the other side hail another cab.' The cat's slipping; I shrug it back up. 'I know it's not a perfect process but it's better than the alternative.'

I look around.

'Where are the twins?'

'Your money bought them a holiday.'

She grabs hold of Imogene's hand, then glares accusingly at me.

'Why can't you get a proper job, Rainbow?'

The cat slips against my torso.

I shrug it back up.

'Sorry, Sal, but this is what I do.'

Chapter 24

BACK FROM THE DEAD

I bump against the pink wing reflector with Cadillac inscribed on the back as I slip into the passenger side of the wheels, the side that the slug with Rory's name on it exited, the side with the brace of Zastava M57 pistols on the seat, and shove them out of the way.

They don't explode.

Surprise.

Zastavas usually explode.

There's a sound like a sick dog gasping but there's nothing under the bench seat but knives and nothing in the glove box, either, if you ignore the dozen dead-men's driving licences and the fifty or so mobile phones, plus three revolvers and a bunch of grenades.

Ditto the back seat, apart from Rory's crutch, a Sokacz sub-machine gun, an Ero nine-millimetre parabellum, an Agram and an APS 95 with optical sights, all of them made in Croatia.

He always was a patriot, Rory.

The gasps ratchet up but there's nothing on his face except surprise and his hands contain only fingerprints.

I finger his pulse and it's then that I discover he's not dead, he's only in shock paralysis after growing a new throat, and that's where the dog's rasps are coming from.

Rube was big on anatomy.

Get on top of the body, she'd tell me, and you're on top of the world – defence, attack, diagnosis, prognosis, post-mortem, ante-mortem, the works.

So I get on top of the body and on top of the body is the

head and the head is perched on the neck and in the neck is the larynx.

The larynx, says *Cunningham's Anatomy* – published 1909 and occupying pride of place on the top shelf in Rube's library between *Ashley's Book of Knots* and *Advanced Forensics* – lies in the interval between the great vessels of the neck.

Hit just about any of these and the possessor is dead – or at least in serious trouble.

But Rory's neither dead nor in serious trouble, just breathing like a sick dog. The marksman hit nothing but the merest whisper of the larynx.

There's got to be an advantage in having a scrawny neck and Rory just found it.

I dig out a handkerchief and wrap it around what's left of his breathing apparatus.

I can't afford to get sprung for driving without a licence.

A thump to the side of the head gets Rory functioning.

He's muttering something about praising the Lord.

Salina appears on the other side of the road with that look still on her face, an overnight bag in one hand and Imogene's paw in the other.

I give Rory another smack over the head.

'Can you drive?'

'How do you think I got here?'

His voice sounds like it's got blood in it.

So does his brain.

'I mean can you drive *now*?' They've reached the gate. 'Can you see straight? Are you compos?'

Rory puts his patella against the steering column, knees himself upright, and fumbles with the ignition.

Salina turns left, dragging the kid after her like a dinghy, and hot-foots it towards the introspection, where she waves away the first cab that comes her way and piles, as instructed, into the second.

'Okay, get going,' I tell Rory.

The eight cylinders burst into pandemonium, most of which bypasses the mufflers. Rory puts his foot down, the car lurches forward, and the armoury in the back of the chariot rattles like a bunch of bones in a graveyard.

The cab carrying Salina and Imogene recedes into the distance.

'What happened?'

I tell Rory what happened and he touches his neck during the telling. It seems only now that he realises a bullet's gone through him.

After I've finished, it's a long time before he answers, and when he does he's raving.

'God meant me to live . . .' The bullet missed his jugular and took out his brain instead. 'But why would anyone want to take a pot at me?'

Wrong question.

Why would anyone *not* want to take a pot at Rory?

He examines his mug in the looking glass, the one with the miniature revolver hanging off it.

'God wanted me to live,' he says again.

Something happened to Rory and it's not just a bullet.

'Forget God,' I tell him, 'and tell me about the gorilla.'

Rory shrugs.

'Well, Gandhi,' he begins and notes my look of incomprehension, 'that's the dog – had a go at him, because the ape was waving his chopper at me, so the ape sank his axe into the dog instead and cleared out, taking the axe with him.'

'Where's the other dog, the one I asked you to look after?'

He tells me Rocket has taken Gandhi's place in his affections and the pooch is safe at home. I ask him how he went with the shopping list, prior to him nearly becoming an item on it himself.

'A couple of years back,' he says, 'I did this little job.'

I nod.

Everyone knows Rory kills people.

'Who was the client?'

'A guy called The Red Dwarf. He was in charge of State Prisons.'

The morning's overcast and behind us there's not much in the way of traffic, while up front there's a hole in the clouds, and I'm beginning to see the light, too.

'So you called in the IOU?'

Rory nods.

'I gave him the name and the photograph you gave me plus the piece of paper with the name of the music teacher on it, plus the prints.'

'And?'

'The prints came up negative. The Jones dude's clean. He's never done time.'

Back to square one.

And in square one I can see, via the wing mirror – the one I knocked crooked when I got in so that it's angled my way rather than towards Rory – nestled amongst all the other vehicles on the road in much the same way that Rory's perforated larynx is nestled in the cluster of muscles, glands and arteries that go to make up his skinny little neck, a vehicle that shouldn't be there: the black cabriolet.

Chapter 25

THE RETURN OF THE
BLACK CABRIOLET

'Turn off here.'

Rory doesn't hear or, if he does, chooses to ignore.

I've unholstered the gat and I'm busy checking that it's got the requisite complement of slugs in its sidecar but Rory sails right on past the turnoff like I haven't said a word.

He might be dumb but he's not deaf.

'Next left.'

But he keeps his foot on the gas feeder and also keeps looking straight ahead, along the long pink bonnet with the Cadillac wreath on the end, focusing on chewing up tar macadam rather than taking orders from passengers.

'If we're stopping at all,' he says, 'we're stopping at McDonald's.'

That's when he looks across at me and that's when he sees the gat.

It's taken him a long time.

It's a big gat.

'What are you doing with the equaliser?'

'We're being followed.'

Rory's never been big on detail.

He goes around with his gun cocked, his attitude in neutral and his brain on safety and when some joker interferes with his lifestyle, he pots them.

Until then he's going for a ride in the country.

'Look, it might have escaped your attention, Rainbow, but we're on a road. And on roads some vehicles are in front of you, some are beside you, and some are going in the opposite direction, while others are behind you, following. It's called traffic.'

My eyes haven't left the looking glass.

'It's the black cabriolet.'

Rory looks where I'm looking.

'That old heap!'

He puts his foot down.

'No way that washing machine can keep up with us, man. This is a Caddie. Know what its engine capacity is? Eight-point-two. Against what?'

He answers his own question.

'A fly's fart.'

I wind down the window.

A typhoon swirls into the Caddie and tickles my trigger finger.

Arguing with Rory is like trying to reason with a stoat.

'Think, Roarer!' I yell at him. 'Use the old grey matter for once and explain to me how that old rattler is keeping up with us, unless it's able to!'

Rory was nervous about being shot even before he got shot.

He takes his foot off the speed dial.

'Okay, but put the cannon away, will you?'

The Caddie lurches into another lane.

The driver of a 120Y protests.

Rory aims the Caddie at him.

The 120Y takes a trip into the forest.

'Look, I admit it, okay?' he croaks, straightening up. 'Guns in the hands of other people make me nervous, because I know what damage they can do.'

Rory's orbs swivel between the road, the cabriolet and the shooter.

'Those things are like magnets. Shoot one and it attracts others, like iron filings in a lab.'

Rube told me Rory was going to become a scientist before he decided to kill for a living.

His teachers were impressed with his talent for pulling the wings off beetles.

Teachers aren't the fastest balls in the cartridge.

'So what do we do now?'

We compromise and we stop at a KFC, that's what we do now, offloading a couple of kids out of a window seat to enable me to surveill the action outside, while at the same time avoiding the sight of the Diet Coke dribbling out of the holes in Rory's neck.

But no black car swings into the KFC parking lot and there's no joker crouching beside the Caddie, looking over his shoulder while he's letting down the tyres or interfering with the steering or taking to the brake lines with a hacksaw.

'I'm sorry I'm late. I've just come from another of those wretched meetings to save the hospital.'

It's two hours later and I've just left Rory to get a visual of David Jones so he can describe him to the Dwarf. I'm on the hillside above the cottage just around the corner from the wombat farm when Sally Kane arrives, smiling out of a flushed face and smoothing down her hair, which is ruffled.

Being back on the mountain is like old times.

I like old times.

You can't get hurt in old times.

'Here's the progress report,' I say. 'On the one hand I've made headway but on the other hand I've made no headway at all.'

Sally Kane's wearing a sheer floral skirt, sensible shoes and a confused expression on her face.

The only thing she's not wearing is her money bag.

'I'm not following you.'

'You might not be but someone else is.'

I tell her about the black cabriolet.

'Someone's after your husband, Dr Kane, and it looks like they don't particularly care for private detectives poking around where it doesn't concern them.'

'Perhaps you should stop poking around, then.'

She's speaking slowly and all the while she's gazing down at the little red-roofed cottage, the one with the shepherd outside tending his sheep.

'It's too late for that, lady. Besides, like I said, I'm making headway.'

There's no point telling her too much.

She's scared enough as it is.

Instead I stick to what might have a direct bearing on the matter.

'On the name thing, I'm drawing a blank – David Jones still hasn't got a history.'

I let that sink in.

'When I ran out of proof that your husband might be having an affair – that is, failed to discover an affairee worthy of the name – I tried the next best reason anyone might have for desiring privacy, and that is that your husband might possess form.'

'What's form?'

Even surgeons can be ignorant.

'Gone down, done time, been inside, soiled his pants –'

'I'm sorry?'

'Been in jail.'

'Oh.'

Sally Kane smoothes down her dress but she doesn't look as surprised as she might be.

'And has he?'

I shake my head.

The Dwarf came up with David Jones's report card and it turned out to be as blank as the prints of a murderer wearing Latex.

'Not a whisper. Not under his own name and not under anyone else's. Hasn't even done an overnighter for speeding.'

Sally Kane goes quiet for a long time after that.

I can't even hear her mind operating.

Clients are strange.

Give them what they want and suddenly they don't want it any more.

'That's it, then,' she whispers.

I move my head by way of a negative.

There's still the black cabriolet.

Plus Rory and the kid nearly copped it. Harriet Stowe and Little Miss Twisty, not to mention Imogene's cat, are dead. And David Jones looks all set to follow in their wake.

'That's not it at all,' I tell her, 'in fact it's not even the beginning. Someone's after your husband and I've got to find out who. And why.'

I don't like loose ends.

They tend to flap around when you least expect it and end up hurting people.

'So you wish to continue your investigations?'

'Wrong auxiliary,' I tell her, 'I've got to keep investigating.'

Sally Kane takes a deep breath and when it comes out it's quavering.

She's changed her mind back again.

Time to apply for a withdrawal.

'I've run out of the necessary.'

Sally Kane smiles.

'I thought you might have.'

She stands and turns away to face the sunset. It's formed an outer ring of rose-pink around a bullseye of madder crimson. I sense that my complexion's acquiring much the same colouration . . . Sally Kane has hitched up her dress with one hand and is fiddling around beneath it with the other. When she finally turns to face me, her eyes are shining, her skirt's caught up, and she's gripping a fistful of fifties.

She notes the question mark in my eyes.

'When one is introduced to a new bank, Mr Scutt,' she says, adjusting her dress as she hands me the dough, 'it doesn't hurt to open an account there, does it?'

Chapter 26

THE CASE OF THE NERVOUS REALTOR

'What do you mean, pulled a gat on you?'

'What do you mean, what do I mean?'

Rory's still got the holes in his neck.

He's also still got the hole in his head where his brain ought to be.

We're on the road back to the City.

It's going to be a long trip.

'Jokers don't just pull gats on people, Roarer.'

'Well, this one did.'

I talk him through his interview with David Jones.

'You open the door.'

'I what?'

'That's what you did, right? Opened the door.'

'Opened what door?'

'The door to the real estate joint.'

'No.'

I try it in low gear, uphill, with the brakes on.

'Look, Roarer, how could you get in, if you didn't open the door?'

'It's a self-opening door.'

'Okay, the door opens all by itself. Then what?'

'This doxy's there.'

Call me old-fashioned but I don't like dames being referred to as doxies.

Dames are dames or they're ladies, unless they're broads.

But I let it pass.

In some respects, Rory's beyond teaching.

'All right, then what happens?'

Then what happens, Rory tells me, is that the doxy comes onto him.

One look at Rory's sea-greens and she's yak-fat in his hands and melting, or that's how Rory describes it. She asks him if he's wearing coloured contact lenses and when he tells her no, she wants to know what happened to his leg. This gives him the green light to make with the story concerning his battle with the great white pointer, armed with nothing more than raw strength, sheer courage, and the shattered tip-end of a mizzen-mast.

That's when the guy appears in the doorway.

When he sees Rory, he turns pale.

'What do you want?' he asks.

Rory rounds on the newcomer, his crutch cocked.

'Who's asking?'

David Jones takes in the naked dame on Rory's T-shirt, the missing leg, plus the wrap around his throat and I begin to understand the gun thing, only I don't tell Rory that, because he's busy negotiating the traffic.

The realtor goes into realtor mode.

'Perhaps you'd be interested in purchasing property.'

Rory forgets the dame and remembers his mission.

'Yeah, perhaps I would.'

'Please come this way.'

Rory lurches after the dude, but not without bestowing a wink on the receptionist as he passes.

The two enter Jones's office and that's when Jones pulls a gun on him.

'Just like that?'

Rory makes like he's busy with the gear stick.

'There might have been a bit of a lead-up.'

'What might have been the lead-up?'

'The guy wanted to know who sent me.'

The skin on the back of my neck prickles.

'You're sitting down, right?'

Rory glances in my direction, wisdom in his eyes but not in his brain.

'How can I draw my gat when I'm sitting down?'

'You drew your gat?'

Rory never had family.

Consequently, when he meets people he tends to shoot them. He finds normal social intercourse challenging.

'You're dead right I drew my gat. The guy had a crack at me.'

'How did he have a crack at you?'

'By asking who sent me.'

'But someone always sends you, Roarer, that's what you do, you get sent, you're a killer.'

Rory's eyes go hard, like the Cadillac wreath on the bonnet is a rifle sight and he'd like to take out the world.

'Let's get this straight, Roarer,' I go on. 'Jones asks who sent you, so you go for your gat only he beats you to the draw.'

'It wasn't in the drawer, it was behind his desk.'

'Describe it.'

'What, the desk?'

'No, the gun.'

'Browning trombone-action rifle, 22 calibre, a pop gun.'

A very nervous and very hunted realtor who's so dead scared for his life he's got a handgun in his study at home and a rifle behind his desk at work.

'What happened then?'

'What happened when?'

'After he pulls the gun on you.'

'I answer the question.'

'You told him I sent you?'

He shakes his head.

'I told him I was there to take care of him.'

Rory's no expert in linguistics.

'He didn't seem to know how to take it. So while he was working out how to take it, I left. I believe God guided both my words and my actions. The receptionist wanted to continue our conversation but I kept right on getting the hell out of there.'

The black car's bouncing around in the wing mirror.

There are three ways you can deal with cars following you.

You can step on the gas and risk getting done by the cops,

not the smartest cut on the breadboard considering the firepower the cops would discover on the back seat.

You can try shooting out the car's tyres. This isn't too smart, either, because given the crate's vintage, the tyres are probably made of solid rubber.

Or you can pretend the tail's not there, sit back, and count the daisies.

There's no choice, so I take it.

Chapter 27

THE RED DWARF

'You got to pull yourself together, Roarer.'

It's mid-afternoon and we're at Rory's.

He's got Rocket on his knee and I've done as much of a debug as I can manage – checked the lightbulb, run my hands over what passes for chairs in Rory's joint and looked under the linoleum. I'm working on the gaps between my teeth with an Interden in the ongoing battle against dental caries. Rory's muttering to himself.

'Man, I just want to put an end to all this killing!' he says. 'I've found God and want to join the Hare Krishnas.'

'That's all very well,' I say, scraping the roach off my shoe with the pointy end of the toothpick before going back to the caries, 'but your conversion will have to wait until the completion of your contract.'

Roarer's eyes have gone murky, like someone just disturbed the seafloor.

'I can no longer be a party to senseless slaughter.'

It's like he senses what's ahead.

'Look,' I say, giving up on the teeth, 'the only guarantee with death is that it happens. But if there are going to be any killings, you won't be the one required to perform them.'

Rory seems satisfied with that, only you can't tell with born agains.

When you least expect it they can turn around and crucify you.

'So what do you want me to do?'

'We call in the IOU from your new best friend, the short person.'

'I've already called it in.'
'So we call it in some more.'
'And I won't be killing anyone?'
'Only if you don't drive careful.'

There's been talk that, as part of his conversion, Rory will be ditching the Caddie.

But it hasn't happened yet, so we take Sydney's potholed Western Highway that becomes The Parramatta Road that in turn becomes Broadway until it magically transforms itself into George Street. We finally reach a joint that's got a porn pedlar in the basement, a religious bookseller on the ground floor, and God knows what in the hereafter.

Rory parks the Caddie and we climb out.

The porn pedlar doesn't look up from behind his counter as we enter.

'Same-sex stuff's up the back.'

'We're not same sex.'

The porn pedlar's travel weary eyes come up off his comic book and crawl over Rory before returning, covered with grime, to me.

'Whatever you say, pal, if you know what I mean.'

Rory comes to the rescue – the porn pedlar's, not mine.

'We need to see Howard.'

Tupperware grimaces.

'I'll see if she's in.'

He presses a bouton.

'Two guys, Kevin,' he says into it, 'only they claim they're not guys, if you know what I mean. Three legs between 'em, the mono's got a crutch rifle, and the biped's packing a gat.'

He listens for a couple of beats then glances at Rory.

'You the killer?'

'I was,' Rory says, 'but I'm not any more, because I found God.'

The dealer squints through his cynicism.

I shove Rory aside.

'Yeah, he's the killer.'

Rory looks puzzled.

'But you told me –'

I shoot him a look, the one with the leg-lopping landmine in it.

'It's just a description, Roarer, okay? They only call you a killer, it doesn't mean it's what you do.'

The porn pedlar's back on the speaker.

'There's a bit of confusion over definitions here, boss.'

I shove him out of the way and grab the phone.

'There's no confusion, Howard, it's Rory all right, just tell us where we can find you and we'll come right on in.'

Kevin Howard's sitting on a stool when we find him and I can see that he's small, even when he's wearing a stool.

He's got hair the colour of a Jaffa, he's wearing a pair of horn rims that Buddy Holly would have been proud of, and he looks like the nervous type.

'What's the problem?' he asks.

'I got two names and I want to know where they came from.'

'Why should I help you?'

'Because you owe Rory and I'm with Rory.'

'I already helped Rory.'

'Then you can help him some more.'

'Maybe I can,' the small man says, 'but I'll need dates, places, names and descriptions.'

So I tell him maybe seven years ago, Sydney, Edith Burton, and I describe her.

I don't tell him David Jones because that's the name of a department store, but Rory describes the joker that wears the moniker.

'What's he done?'

What's he done, this husband of yours? I asked Sally Kane.

And Sally Kane replied: Nothing.

'Nothing,' I tell Kevin Howard, 'but someone wants to do him harm and I need to know why.'

'So why come to me?'

'Because everyone else that can help us is dead.'

'Does that mean I might go the same way?'

'Only if you're not careful.'

'Death's a high price to pay for helping people.'

I shoot him a look.

'You ought to know all about that.'

The Dwarf sighs and climbs down from his stool.

You can see how he scored the cognomen.

'You're right.' He pauses. 'Look, there's not much small people can do in this world except work in circuses, and the do-gooders are making even that difficult, because they claim that working in circuses is some sort of exploitation.'

He waits for me to say something, only I don't say anything, so he goes on.

'Because of these self-same do-gooders I had to give up my cushy number as a clown, because the circus I was in had a management you might describe as weak-willed, however through sheer perseverance and ability I was able to forge a highly successful career in the public service instead.

'Consequently, I found myself in charge of State Prisons and on the shortlist – all right, I've heard all the jokes – to become head of the Federal Department of Immigration.'

The Dwarf's expression turns sour.

'That's when the bastard who was supposed to retire duds me and decides he's not going to retire, after all.'

He stares out the window.

I don't know what he's seeing.

It can't be the view, because the sill's at least a foot higher than his head.

'Accordingly, I get Rory to top him.'

Rory moans.

Any man's death diminishes him, or at least his chance of getting into Heaven.

Outside a bell tolls and the way Rory looks it tolls for him.

'Rory stands in front of the limo and machine guns the dude as he's coming down the driveway of his Vaucluse mansion. He also takes out the chauffeur, and that wasn't even in the contract.'

Rory moans again, or maybe he's just praying.

'The trouble with taking out the chauffeur is it leaves no one steering the Rolls, as a consequence of which the vehicle runs into Rory, who's standing in the gateway clutching his equaliser, like Cary Grant in *High Noon*.'

'Gary Cooper.'

The Dwarf arrives back at the stool and somehow gets himself back up onto it again.

'Whatever. Anyway, I'm behind this bush making sure Rory does the job and that's how I see Rory get himself crunched between the limo and the cast-iron gatepost. I drag him free and that's when I tell him I owe him.'

He contemplates the desk.

'Of course, that's not going to bring the leg back, despite the best efforts, et cetera, et cetera.' His glasses look like they're in danger of misting over. 'Anyhow, the upshot was the stiff was dead, we framed someone for it, Rory lost a leg and I got the job.

And when I retired, the payout from a grateful government was enough to set me up for life.'

He looks at Rory and the look he gives him is one of the deepest gratitude.

'Which means I owe Rory, and accordingly I'll do whatever he asks. I still possess the necessary contacts.'

By the time I get Rory out of there he's a mess.

'This all relies on me being a killer.'

'Don't worry, Roarer,' I tell him, 'life's not a retrospective.'

The bell tolls again and it belongs to the little stone church across the way. The tolling reminds Rory that his way to Heaven is paved with more potholes than the Great Western Highway. He asks if I'd mind leaving him alone for a while before turning and crutch-and-one-legging it across the road. The last I see of him (until the next time I see him) is a small, lonely, lopsided figure making its way towards the church, the common and garden variety traffic veering and honking and crashing around him.

Only it's not your common and garden variety traffic, because one of the vehicles in it is the black cabriolet.

Chapter 28

THE HOOD WITH NO HANDS

In a world without answers, the cabriolet is what comes after the question mark.

It trundles through the first batch of lights headed for Park, and I make off after it.

I'm not in peak condition, what with one or a hundred whiskies too many, and I can see that the traffic's not in the mood to cooperate.

But you don't solve cases waiting for traffic to cooperate.

Alice in Wonderland is showing in the movie parlours in George Street and kids are queued twenty-deep on the trottoir to see it.

I leap two of the ankle-biters but two more don't make it because they bob up their heads at the wrong time.

A mother voices a protest but I'm up for the greater good.

A geezer in a wheelchair hits the turf.

An old dame whirls like a top and follows him.

A couple of schoolgirls go down.

Collateral damage is never a good thing but sometimes it can't be avoided.

By City Hall, I'm close enough to the chariot to see the reflection in the windows of the joker chasing it.

It's clutching its hat and G-forces have got hold of its face as the boneshaker slows down to make the turn into Park and I make the leap.

The breath is punched out of me as my body thumps into the paintwork and I grab the nearside door pillar while the soles of my whitesides make contact with the running-board.

I need an ID.

There's only one way to make an ID under the circumstances, so I take it.

Sirens are headed our way, a wing-beater's fluttering overhead and the cabriolet's doing fifteen paces per second, not the speed of lightning in raw tabulation but sound-barrier stuff when you're clinging to a running-board.

It's now or forever.

My toes forming the fulcrum, I clench the bo-peeps, throw my body weight onto the ankle joints, in the same nanosecond placing my hands in the thumbs-in-fingers-out position. Someone inside chucks open the back-hinged door, which is when I adjust for the rear-thrust of relativity and back-arch over the hatch. I force my feet towards the bow to ensure the footwear lands on the running-board. At the same time, I drop into a full crouch, twist my head, and flick open my eyes, the rods and cones having had time to adjust during the hand-spring, in order to obtain a spot-check of the cabriolet's interior.

A glance is all I need.

Resist obvious identifiers, Rube always told me, hair can be cut, irises discoloured, and beards purchased at the nearest theatrical supply shop.

That's why hoods scowl.

Witnesses can remember the expression but not the perpetrator, to the ultimate benefit of the perpetrator, because next time they see him he's smiling.

I do the ID.

Squatting in the cabriolet's bucket seats are two figures in black, between them packing enough weaponry to make the pre-conversion Rory look like a pacifist — sawn-off shotgun, sub-machine pistols, mortars, handguns, a howitzer, everything but an ack-ack battery, and I can't even swear to them not possessing that.

Clothes can be changed and weapons are little more than fashion-accessories.

Therefore observe such factors as shoulder slope, face geometry, length of leg, hands.

I check accordingly.

Passenger: Baby-faced, hunched shoulders, big hands.

Driver: Regulation scar on cheek, shoulders squared, no hands.

I blink in the darkness.

Rods and cones playing tricks.

I look again, staring despite the pain in the fist where Babyface has grabbed hold of me.

But the driver's still got no hands, nothing but a couple of black coat-cuffs ending in two angry red stumps where the hands should be.

The case of the missing mana distracts me when I shouldn't have let it.

I wrench my fist free from Babyface and bang him over the skull. Too late I remember the bazooka and by the time my brain starts functioning again, the joker's had time to work out his counter move, bringing the weaponry back as far as he can. He rams it into my solar plexus, the result being my ribs hurt that much more, my lungs are deprived of breath, my blood finds itself deoxygenated, my brain swims, I experience vertigo, and I fall off the running-board.

Rube used to refer to it as cinematographic time warp but these days they just call it Fast Forward. This is exactly what the chariot does when I come off the running-board. I roll in the dust at the feet of a broad in red leotards who's standing on the corner of Denizen and William, smiling at passers-by as she enjoys a quiet cigarette preliminary to whatever she might be thinking of doing next. Meanwhile the cop cars close in and the eggbeater swoops low and I get to my feet, pick up the gat, reinstall my fedora, nod to the dame and take myself off towards the traffic tunnel.

I'm running from the cops.

But I'm also trying to shake the image of the handless hood in the cabriolet.

Chapter 29

INCIDENT AT ALCATRAZ

The tunnel's not built for pedestrians but the other thing going for it is there's no entry for choppers either. The whoomph-whoomph-whoomph of the eggbeater fades to yesterday amid the roar of the klaxons and the squeal of brakes as I head past the GO BACK YOU'RE GOING THE WRONG WAY signs and start burrowing underground.

I hang onto the hat and hug the wall as I hammer my way along the right-hand side of the carriageway.

The way to survive, Rube taught me, is not just to keep moving, but to keep the cerebrum humming along while you're doing it.

How do you survive?

Keep thinking, I'd tell her.

Good boy, she'd reply.

And I'd get a tot of the vodka.

In tunnels, the cops have got two sources of intelligence – the cameras on the walls and the jokers on their mobiles dialling 131700 and screaming there's a maniac loose in their tunnel.

The trick is to get them in synch and get them wrong.

The cameras are predictable.

What is also predictable is that lights start flashing and the electronic signs start purveying the false information that there's an accident ahead, so as not to unduly excite the populace, and drivers are kindly requested to throw out the anchors.

What is unpredictable is the pale-green Vespa wobbling through the stalled traffic, the rider in the matching green helmet ignoring all instructions to stop, which is the whole point of Vespas, until I appear in front of it waggling my arms and looking official, thereby causing it to squeak to a halt, at which time I dislodge the rider from his perch and take over the conveyance.

The pain in my mitt incurred during the incident with the jalopy has eased and I manage to control the two-wheeler with one hand as I manoeuvre it between the stalled traffic while gripping onto the fedora with the other. By the time the cops can get even close to realising what's on, I'm out of the southern exit of the tunnel and sliding into South Dowling and the maze of streets that go to make up Slurry Hills. I lose the Vespa before we become too attached to each other, under a tree that's pretty much the same colour as the scooter.

From then on it's hoof-time.

I've remembered the address of my old ballet teacher and that's where I make for: sub-unit 2960 on the twenty-ninth level of one thousand, two hundred and twenty-three-B Cortizone. It's an above-ground bomb shelter constructed along much the same lines as the hotel in California called Alcatraz, otherwise known as a New South Wales Housing Commission hell-hole. There are job lots of artificial greenery in pink plastic pots gracing the darker corners of the bricked-in balconies, to add that extra little touch of sheer fun to the surroundings.

The eggbeater's a distant memory as I reach the balcony of the twenty-ninth floor. I catch my breath and hammer with my good fist on the imitation wood door of sub-unit three-sixty, in the space between the cracked eye-peeper, the broken door handle, and infinity.

No one answers.

There's no eggbeater around so why am I experiencing this sudden feeling of panic?

It must be the surrounds, trapped as I am in a rabbit warren three hundred feet above ground zero, with nothing about me but unpainted concrete, plastic pot plants, and a lot of depression.

'Who's there?'

Who do they think's here, the Avon lady?

I tell them it's the cops and the door opens just enough to reveal a chain, an eye and a waft of foul air.

'You're not the cops,' the eye tells me.

'And you're not Madam Blavatsky.'

'Weirdo,' the eye says.

And the door slams in my face.

I make an attempt at a laugh.

Rube always told me that laughing is miles ahead of the alternative so I'm still laughing as I turn, shaking my head and rubbing the back of the mitt as I do so.

But when I raise my eyes it's to discover, standing between me and the fake pot plants and twenty-nine storeys of stratosphere, someone I don't particularly want to see. The hood with no hands. And he's holding the howitzer and it's pointing right at the place where I was laughing.

Chapter 30

THE MAD DOG

The scar on the cheek under the homburg looks like it's been excavated by a meat cleaver, the mouth is bitter gall, and the eyes are ashes. It's the eyes that stop me going for the gat. These eyes go back to the beginning of Time, when Neanderthals trembled in caves, things were alive that had no business being alive, and death crept abroad after nightfall. In these eyes hate has shoved aside reason. The irises are opaque, they're crawling with malevolence the way a long-interred corpse writhes with worms, and they're craving pain – other people's – because a quick death would be merciful, the sort of hate that needs to hear the screams of its victims echoing throughout all eternity.

Scarface waggles the tip of the howitzer. 'Move,' he murmurs.

There's no opening and closing of the mouth to indicate speech, I can't even be sure he's spoken, but I know what he wants, so I move.

It's a long way to the ground when you've started on the twenty-ninth floor, you're being forced to take the fire escape, and you've got a howitzer gouging into your back, held by a handless killer.

Don't ask me how he's holding it, it's not something I want to think about.

There's not much more light in the stairwell than there is in the eyes of the killer and I've got to rely on my whitesides to tell me there's several dead rats, a broken chair, and a job lot of what look like discarded body parts to negotiate on the way down.

At my back I hear the soft whisper of the hood's footfalls, and in case I think it's just noises there's the ongoing thrust between my shoulder blades of the business end of the howitzer.

I wait until the ninth before making my move.

There's a split-second when the hood finds himself caught up in a Queen-sized Sleepmaker Rest-Assured with a syringe sticking out of it. Meanwhile, I'm two steps down, and there's no guarantee I'll find myself with another chance like this one.

I feint to the left, do a double-turn with twist ending in a forward-thrust somersault, and the cannon goes off while I'm in mid-air and dropping, the thunder of its percussion hammering at my lugs as it smacks a crater the size of a baby's skull in the reinforced concrete wall of the stairwell, a millimetre away from my neck.

I keep going, because there's nothing else to keep.

Being handless doesn't slow the killer, who's busy redefining Ness's logic of movement at the same time as he's redeploying gravity, ricocheting off the sides of the fire stairs like a one-man avalanche as he tumbles down the companionway after me.

By the penultimate landing, my breath is searing my throat and the maniac's gaining, the clatter of his hoofbeats just one step behind my starboard Achilles tendon. Fast running out of options, I make the final turn to the exit and the promise of a taste of freedom.

It's then that I realise my mistake.

I've been focusing on the threat behind me.

Focusing's good because it concentrates the energy, at a time when the energy needs to be focused.

But it can also be bad, on account of it blinkers you to any danger that might be waiting for you elsewhere.

And it's bad now because before me and blocking my escape route, a mangy cur of a dog cringing beside him, is the second hood, the baby-faced one, and he's holding a submachine gun, the gat with the round-box magazine, the infamous M1928A1. It's the very gun that Al Capone's hoods used on that fateful St Valentine's Day all of eighty years ago. The baby-faced hood is smiling because such a simple trick has worked, and he likes simple tricks, in fact, the simpler the better.

I'm a rabbit at the mouth of a warren, there's a ferret fore and aft, and both have got their razor teeth bared and scalpel claws out, all set to tear me apart.

'Don't!'

It's Babyface, it's a baby's voice, and it's not addressed to me, but to the killer behind me with the howitzer.

'I said don't!' he squeaks again.

I sense the thug at my back park the machinery.

Babyface returns his attention to me.

'Unbutton your jacket.'

It's like open-heart surgery without the anaesthetic.

Babyface tucks the Thompson into one mitt, smacks me across the skull with the other fist, and relieves me of the Smith & Wesson, flicking the shells out one-handed before parking the gat inside his suit, never taking his eyes off me for a moment.

The mutt looks on with interest.

'Now the blade.'

The hood bends, removes the dagger from my shin scabbard with the gat-free mitt and tosses it onto the garbage heap that is Alcatraz's backyard. Then he straightens, all in the one movement, like he's just smacked a mosquito, pinched it between his fingernails, and is negligently disposing of the remains.

'The hat.'

I pass him the fedora.

He knows where the second blade is and how to remove it without cutting himself.

He also knows something else.

'Now the hand.'

Something clicks in my brain.

Somewhere deep in my subconscious, from the moment I came fascia to ugly mug with Handless Hood on the balcony, I've been trying to work out how they tracked me.

Now I know.

It's like Hank said: Why worry about people's location when you can plant a bug on them?

I hand over the mitt, the one that Babyface whacked in the cabriolet, the one I've been nursing ever since, the way you'd nurse a hand that's been bitten by a tarantula.

The hood's gripping the blade between thumb and forefinger.

It's a double-edger, hollow-honed blue-steel with the name Eversharp inscribed on the side, so you know what to ask for when you want a replacement, an Escher vase cut-out in the middle for fitting a hand-grip to, on the off-chance you might want it for shaving.

Babyface doesn't.

He grips my paw and it's not just because he's suffering a sudden attack of the friendlies.

Blood spurts out of the hand as he slices and the pain's severe, but I can do pain.

I watch as the thug disentangles the technology with the same degree of compassion that a vet might display removing a blood-filled tick from a horse.

The technology's small and black and when inserted under the epidermis, enables a follower to track the hand, plus anything else that happens to be attached to it.

'Here, boy!'

Babyface is addressing the cur.

The mutt wriggles excitedly, waggling its tail because it thinks that for once in its miserable life it's found a friend. Instead of patting the dog, the thug reaches down and with one deft movement tucks the bug in next to the mutt's right eyeball, just beside the tendo-palpebrarum.

The dog screams, spins wildly and careers down the rutted road, yipping and bleating and leaping in circles, the sound of its agony providing a suitable accompaniment to the murmur of approval from the thug with the baby's face and the torturer's heart. Soon enough, the animal has disappeared over the edge of the rubbish-strewn horizon.

But there's no time for empathy.

Babyface has got both mitts back on the gat and is motioning with it like he'd much prefer pulling the trigger to employing it as a pointer.

'Move!' he squeaks.

I move.

The second hood's beside me but I don't look in his direction because I haven't been invited and in these circumstances you only do what you're invited to do, as per Lesson Thirty-Seven in Aunt Rube's Manual of Survival.

The landscape around Alcatraz is all that was left in *The Book of Revelation* after the Angels of the Lord paid their little visit to a sinful world – nothing but bleak black towers and straggling weeds and bottomless pits and desolation and death and eternal misery.

In normal circumstances, it's just such a landscape that hoods like these would choose to do their killing in.

They are Book of Revelation people.

Only these circumstances aren't normal.

Because if they were, the hoods would already have done their killing.

Instead they prod me across the blighted landscape and when I stumble they force me upright and instead of exxing me they push me forward.

Nothing stirs in the black towers.

Seething tens of thousands of condemned souls dwell here but in the harsh light of day, with two black-suited and heavily-armed hoods conducting an abduction, the denizens are so many craven figures trembling behind blinds, primitive beings cowering in caves in the presence of forces they don't understand, offering this ritual sacrifice to the gods, namely me.

My gun and my blades are gone, but it's the bug I miss.

There was something comforting about it, like it offered the solace of ethereal attachment, even if that attachment was only a malevolent one.

But now even that comfort has been stripped from me, leaving me naked.

The hood screams, 'Forward!'

Hugging my bleeding paw to my bruised ribs, I manage to stumble into a trot.

123

Chapter 31
A CRIMINAL CONVERSATION

There's not much room left in a cabriolet after you've factored in two hoods, the armoury, a suitcase, the victim, and the body odour.

The handless hood is at the wheel.

Don't ask me how he works the gear stick, probably the same way he picks his nose, and while he's playing his ultimate computer game – tracking the final agony-stricken-journey-to-madness of the dog via the GPS on the dashboard – he's giggling.

In the back with me, the hood with the hands has ripped off my fedora and forced a balaclava over my head, backwards, and tied my hands between my knees. He's joined them to my neck with a slip knot in the time honoured manner of the criminal conspiracy, so that if I move at all, the noose around my neck tightens, and if I move any more than that, I'm history.

I fight down the panic.

Have one bad experience and it comes back to haunt you.

Have a second bad experience and it never goes away.

But bad memories never got anyone anywhere so I concentrate on the problem in hand.

Rube on logic:

Pick a number, double it, take away the number you first thought of, and what you're left with is the answer.

In other words: Follow your hunch. So I follow my hunch.

And my hunch is that if I hang around these two roosters much longer, I'm chalk.

These hoods are the psychopaths of my childhood, grown to maturity.

They eat, sleep, drink, fornicate, defecate, urinate, pick their noses, and kill people.

They've climbed dripping from their primaeval swamp, loped to Chicago's O'Hare Airport and flapped like a pair of pterodactyls to the Antipodes. They've then got hold of a souped-up jalopy and topped up their small arms collection. They didn't come all this way for the good of their health or anybody else's, because they've only got one thing on their minds – apart from eating, sleeping, drinking, fornicating, defecating, urinating, and picking their noses – and that is killing people.

I stress-test my bonds.

The action is rewarded with a tightening of the noose and a crack over the skull with the butt-end of the armoury.

I try reasoning.

'You got the wrong guy,' I tell the upholstery.

All I get for that is another crack over the skull.

You learn to listen in this game.

You got to separate the whisky from the water, the angel dust from the talc, the sand from the gunpowder.

They're taking me somewhere and I need to know where and I also need to know why.

And I'm not going to get to know any of that by asking.

Accordingly I make like I'm in the Land of Nod.

'That banana giving you any trouble?'

It's the handless one, the joker driving the jalopy.

They've done their fast-food stop and chomped through a Family-Pak from McDonald's and par consequence the interior of the cabriolet stinks like a soup kitchen in the middle of a summer heat wave.

Babyface gives me a thump.

I don't move.

'Nah, he's dead to the world.'

'Whadya say?'

'It's an expression, idiot. It means he's asleep.'

'Why didnja say so then?'

'Same reason I haven't told you why we're going to Dashiell.'

I can hear the rumble of the supercharged motor and the clash of the weld-hardened gears and the torque of the reinforced crankshaft but for a couple of semesters there's nothing from either of the hoods but breathing.

Then:

'Why are we going to Dashiell?'

Babyface gives me another thump.

I don't respond.

'Because that's where the answer lies, dummy. Remember we asked the boys to do the research, after the court decided to hand out the dough?'

'We wasn't happy.'

'Yeah, like you say, we wasn't happy. Meanwhile, the research resulted in a name, Dashiell. And when we Googled the name in the prison library, we were given the choice between a dead scribbler's moniker and an Australian country town. We took the town.'

'That's when we escaped.'

'And why did we escape?'

'To go to Dashiell.'

'And what did we find when we got to Dashiell?'

'A nosy detective.'

'And what did we do after we found the nosy detective?'

'We followed him.'

Babyface sits back.

'So what we're doing now' – there's satisfaction in his voice – 'is doing our sums.'

'And what sums might they be?'

'We're putting one and one together and coming up with the answer to our little problem, that's what they might be.'

The answer seems to satisfy Handsfree, but I still don't know raspberries from rhubarb.

Chapter 32

A MOUTHFUL OF BLOOD

A couple of hours later the cabriolet hits the dirt.

I need to relieve myself only I figure I'm not about to be handed a toilet pass.

My ribs and the mitt are killing me but that's better than the hoods doing the job.

We pull up six hundred beats after the dirt starts. Babyface rips off the balaclava and removes the strangler-ropes, I get pushed out, a cock crows, there's a shot, the crowing stops, Handsfree sprouts a couple of hooks and picks up the portmanteau, and I get shoved forward.

You don't need to be a genius to work out where we are or what my fate's likely to be or that the clouds covering the sun are cumulo-nimbus.

What I don't know – in relation to the first two questions, at any rate – is why.

Apart from the dead poultry and another fowl or three still in the land of the living, I make out the rusty plough, the shack with the solar panels on it and several acres of wombat holes, any one of which could provide a convenient resting place for a dead detective.

'Why are we here?'

I'm not being existential.

'Because you led us here when we were following you, so we figured this place will lead us to our quarry – move!'

The hood with the hands encourages me into the residence with a clout over the back of the head with the Uzi.

Inside is a chair with arms on it, a table, and the absolute guarantee of a great deal of pain.

Handsfree tables the suitcase, Babyface shoves me into the chair, straps my wrists down with the ropes he's brought from the cabriolet, and stands back.

'All right, punk' – the squeak has risen to a screech – 'where is he?'

It's a good question.

I glance behind me.

Using his meathooks, Handless has opened the lid of the portmanteau.

The hooks look like they're carved out of somebody's grandmother and the portmanteau looks like the sort of box they store evil in.

I answer the question.

'He's behind me, removing his makeup from his handbag.'

Babyface force-feeds me the butt end of the Uzi.

'I asked you a question, punk,' he reminds me, 'where is he?'

I clear my throat.

It's not easy keeping up your end of the conversation with a mouthful of blood.

'Where's who?'

'Waddaya mean, wear shoe?'

I spit out a tooth.

'ID me, you moron, and tell me who you're talking about, on account of I don't happen to possess extra-sensory perception.'

I've regressed forty years, shouting idiocies back at the kids bullying me in the schoolyard.

'Waddaya mean, extra-cents-whatever-you-said?'

'I need a name, idiot.'

The hood's face clears.

Scarface has appeared beside him, he's chewing on a cheroot, and he's fitting together the contents of the suitcase.

He's also handed Babyface what I identify as the ingredients for a thumbscrew.

Suddenly I need to get out of there fast, and it's not just to go to the toilet.

'You expect us to believe you don't know?'

It's like we're playing join-the-dots, except the pencil needs sharpening, a lot of the dots are missing, and someone's mixed up all the numbers.

I tear my attention away from the joker with the hooks, and direct it instead to Babyface.

I need to focus on something.

There are too many memories, all of them bad.

'How did you guess?'

Babyface raises the gat, and it's not just to air-condition the barrel.

'Looks like we got ourselves a wise guy.'

It's not meant as a compliment, because in this fidget's lexicon a wise guy would rank somewhere below a disease-carrying sewer rat and just above the common earthworm.

'If I was a wise guy,' I tell him, 'I wouldn't be strapped to a chair facing certain death at the hands of a couple of goons with their brains missing.'

The sophistry earns me another crack over the skull with the firearm.

'I still don't know what you're talking about,' I manage through the blood.

That's when he tells me what he's talking about.

'Grimaldi,' he squeaks, his lips clenched. 'That bastard Josef Grimaldi.'

It's like some character has wandered into the wrong narrative entirely.

I tell the turnip I don't know what he's talking about, that, in a present day context anyway, I've never heard of Grimaldi, Josef or otherwise, and the name means as much to me as Gruyere, Sobrani, Camembert or Grana Lombardo.

That's when I do a recheck of Captain Hook's handiwork.

Not many punters are familiar with even the most common instruments of torture, because torture's not a commonplace occurrence in the everyday byplay of generally accepted social intercourse in this country.

Members of the John Q. Public, for instance, might imagine that quirt's an activity involving water, a flagellum's what citizens run halfway up a pole after an assassination, and a kurbash is something you do to a dog.

Show them a trebuchet, branks, iron maiden, scarpines, or a bed of Procrustes, and they could be excused for thinking they're seeing a no-longer-extant form of parlour game.

Only going by what Screwjaw's got his hooks into, these babies aren't looking for someone to make up a third in a game of tiddlywinks.

The modern-day rack has dispensed with the old labour-intensive cogs and ratchets and crank handles and pulleys.

Instead it's powered electrically.

Handless is kneeling on the floor beside Babyface attempting to assemble such a contrivance.

I'm hoping he doesn't get it together in a hurry, because all I've got going for me are two things:

The time I can filch from the hoods; and

The vulnerability of the knots that are holding me.

Chapter 33

THE BED OF PROCRUSTES

Aunt Rube taught me three ways of dealing with torture – fight it, ignore it, or avoid it.

I start with the fight.

'You idiots wouldn't have heard of Procrustes.'

There's no answer.

Babyface is having trouble with the thumbscrew and Handsfree's busy at the wall flicking switches.

'I'll take that as a no,' I say into the silence, 'in which case I'll have to tell you.'

Talking is keeping my mind off what they're intending to do to me.

Meantime, I'm working at the knots.

There's got to be some advantage in being a sailor.

'Procrustes, Damastes, Polypemon or simply Procoptas, take your pick, was the name of the world's first sadist.'

Two knots down, four to go.

'You two would have loved him, on account of you're his direct descendants. He'd hammer people out like he was flattening horseshoes, or he'd lop bits off them, in order to fit them into one of two beds he possessed, a short one and a long one.'

'Shuddup!'

Babyface has unfolded a sheet of paper with writing and pictures on it and he's spread it out on the floorboards next to the pieces for the thumbscrew. He's trying to read what's written in the semi-darkness caused by the cloud cover and scratching his head at the same time.

It's not making him any smarter.

'Procrustes possessed a rack much like the one that our idiot friend's put together.'

'I said, shuddup!'

I don't shuddup on account of shudding up's no longer an option.

'Where did you get the torture ware? Ikea? Or maybe it's a flat-pack from Bunnings and you're having trouble making sense of the instructions.'

I get a back-hander for that.

But I'm used to back-handers.

I continue with the ropes.

'Maybe you can't even read.'

Hit a sore spot.

I like hitting sore spots.

'Look, dickhead,' Babyface says. 'I ain't got no trouble reading nothing when it's written in American.'

He thumps the paper.

'Ring circle box-frame twice.'

He shakes his head.

'Call that American?'

I shrug.

'Buy cheap rubbish and you get cheap rubbish instructions.'

Scarface is hammering at the wall-switch with one of his meat hooks.

'Hey, I've found the problem!'

'What is it?'

'There's no power!'

'Try plugging it in.'

'It is plugged in!'

'Switch it on, then.'

'It is switched on!'

Babyface looks out the window then back at Scarface.

He's shaking his baby face.

'Didn't you happen to notice something when we came in, you moron? That this is a solar house and there just happens to be a heap of clouds covering the power supply?'

Scarface resorts to basics.

'You calling me stupid?'

'Well, you're the idiot that got his hands cut off.'

That stops Handsfree.

He's got his hooks raised like Freddie Krueger in one of his moods and he looks like he's ready to give his pal a bit of a scratch-up. That's when he glances in my direction and that's when he lowers them.

He's already got his victim.

One more would only confuse things.

I try bravado.

'What are you going to try now, idiot, Chinese burns?'

Scarface moves closer and he's making a noise like there's a fishhook jagged in his gills.

It can only mean one thing and that is I'm not likely to get out of here in one piece, even with only three knots to go.

'So we just wait for the sun to come out,' he says softly. 'Now why don't you fill in the down time by telling us how you got yourself a stupid name like Rainbow?'

I make like I don't hear him.

'I suppose it came out of some stupid weather report, like the clouds.'

I shrug; the shrug loosens the ropes a little more.

Telling the story will buy time, so I tell it.

'You're half right. My parents were hippies and the day I was born the weather was uncertain.'

I feel like I'm reciting my prayers, and maybe I am.

'There was sun plus a few clouds and my mother could see the resultant phenomenon, on account of she was in a dam at the time.'

Babyface is still trying to assemble the thumbscrew, but I've got Captain Hook's attention.

'What was she doing in a dam?'

I glance at Babyface.

The thumbscrew's a basic instrument of torture – a G-section fits over the thumb, a clamp attaches the machinery to the furniture, and the operator works the screw down into the victim's thumb at his leisure.

I concentrate on the knots holding my right arm.

'Giving birth,' I tell him, 'it's what hippies do.'

Babyface has turned the G-section of the thumbscrew around and if he applies it like that, while the thumbscrew won't work precisely like it was meant to, it will still work.

'She was going through an American Indian phase at the time.'

'Hey, give up on the electrics and get yourself over here!'

Scarface does like he's told, clamping my left wrist with one of his hooks while Babyface removes the rope holding my left radius and ulna to the arm of the chair and attaches the end of the upside-down thumbscrew to my thumb.

I'm down to one knot and after I've untied that the only thing holding me to the chair will be a failure of willpower – and the thumb.

I keep talking.

'She'd heard that Indians named kids after whatever was occurring at the time of their birth.'

The screw starts biting into the nail.

I clench what's left of my teeth and continue.

'And when I came into the world, what was occurring was an arc de ciel over the eastern horizon, also known as a rainbow.'

The screw has got through to the quick.

The device might have been put together upside-down and back-to-front but it's still working.

The only thing it's not doing is holding my wrist to the arm of the chair.

Nothing but the thumb's doing that.

The last knot's proving stubborn.

'That's how I got the name Rainbow. Meanwhile, talking of stupid,' I manage, 'how did you come by the conveyance?'

'What conveyance?'

'The straightback, horseless carriage, voiture, crate, landaulet, wheels, the cabriolet.'

Babyface turns the screw some more and the pain bites into my thumb some more. Scarface's eyes cloud over like the sun, not with any pain he might be experiencing, but because of mine.

I gouge at the knot.

'We needed wheels,' he murmurs, watching the blood seep out from my nail, 'and some punk possessed a hotted-up jalopy. He happened to be in jail at the time so the wheels were on offer.

We took him up on the offer.'

The blood's starting to trickle and now it's my eyes that are clouding.

'Now for the last time, you lowlife punk,' Scarface says softly, 'where's Grimaldi?'

I don't even know who Grimaldi is, much less where.

And because I don't know, if I sit here much longer, the sun will come out, the electrics will come back on, the stretcher will start working, and they'll strap me onto it and start chopping bits off me. I'm going to die and my death will be a long way from easeful.

But there's something neither of these roosters knows.

I've suffered pain like none of their victims could ever have suffered pain before. I suffered it at the hands of sadists much sadder than these punks could ever be and I suffered it young. Apart from all the foregoing, I'm a great believer in adages.

Especially the one that goes, What doesn't kill you makes you stronger.

I've undone the last knot.

My life is hanging by a thumb.

It's time to bid that portion of my anatomy adieu.

Chapter 34

AT LEAST THE COCK DIED CROWING

I don't like impotence, never have.

At least the cock died crowing.

I steady the pulse rate, flex the recta femora, tense the gastrocs, and focus my attention on the seat of the chair, because that's going to provide my fulcrum.

I hear the bone snap and the flesh tear and feel a spear of pain like no other I have ever experienced as I yank my mitt skywards.

It helps that Babyface put the thumbscrew on wrong because it means my wrist's unshackled and I've just got the one joint to pull free.

I leave half my thumb decorating the chair.

It doesn't matter.

It's just another joint.

I hurl myself at the hoods and go straight into a tumble turn, at the last moment switching to a one-hundred-and-eighty-degree spin. I end up two paces away, hunched in a full crouch, what's left of my thumb dribbling gore.

I assess what's left of the situation.

The hoods have gone for their guns.

Professionals anticipate and these two are nothing if not professional.

After the gymnastics, they expect more, so I don't give them more, holding the squat for half a beat longer than they expect me to. The first volley goes wide, converting the front door into splinters and going by the sound effects also taking out another rooster.

Then the hoods do like I know they will: they close ranks.

It's what professionals do.

Faced with a common enemy they go back-to-back.

It makes them a much nicer target than the one they'd provide separate and a lot better target than the one I'm giving them.

I'm supposed to retreat but in this game you don't do what you're supposed to.

Accordingly I shift my weight to my toes and take a flying leap straight at the goons.

One of my whitesides hits nasal cartilage and I've got good cobblers, which is where I catch the second one – a direct hit in the awls.

I don't like brutality, never have.

So I keep it to a minimum.

On a count back – apart from the shattered nose and the manhood problem – there's a broken wrist, half an ear gone, a splintered tibia, a broken rib, a couple of teeth that will never chew on a stogie again and, in one case, temporary paralysis.

There isn't much left to tie up, but after I tourniquet the forearm and wrap what's left of the thumb to stop it haemorrhaging, I drag the hoods outside and attach them – using number eight wire, almost thick enough to make a stiletto with – to the plough.

They're not knots a hangman would be proud of but they'll have to do.

I dig my gat out of Babyface's wardrobe and the fedora from the jalopy, park the gat, reblock the hat, jam it on my head, and return my attention to the hoods.

Scarface is getting his brain back from its visit to the cleaners, but the other one – the babyfaced one with the hands, the shattered manhood and the paralysis – is still out cold, cuddled up to the plough like he's married to it.

I tell Scarface there's more where that came from.

They're not words I'd use normally but this isn't normally.

Plus, I don't want there to be any confusion in the matter.

Scarface requests that I not punish him any more. I tell him I'll accede to his request given his continued cooperation, to which he says he'll try, and I tell him he'd better do better than try unless he wants to be further adjusted, to which he says words to the effect of, Please don't hit me.

It's enough of an introduction for two people just getting to know each other. Accordingly, I figure it's time to advance the dialogue.

'I know what you are and I don't need to know who you are.' I put on my American president look, the one that says I'll stop at nothing to save the world, even if it means destroying most of it in the process. 'What I need to know is *why*.'

'Why what?'

My nod takes in the shack and what has just occurred in it.

'Why the torture, bean brain?'

Handsfree wipes his nose on the plough, which gives me the answer to the nose-picking problem, but only when he's tied to a plough.

'We needed a few answers.'

It's a reply, only it's not the right one.

'We all need answers, but we don't go around torturing people to get them.'

'I mean concerning Grimaldi.'

As well as the shooting lessons and the Cagney movies, home schooling a la Rube included some of the gentler arts, which is how I know Grimaldi's the name of a clown that was around all of two hundred years ago.

'What's a dead clown got to do with the price of thumbscrews?'

But the hood's eyes have gone blank and I can see there aren't going to be any more answers in the immediate future, so I borrow his mobile and make a call.

Chapter 35

DESTINATION WITH DARKNESS

'What happened to your thumb?'

'I put it somewhere it wasn't wanted. But I'm not here to talk about thumbs. Tell me what you know about Josef Grimaldi.'

I've left the hoods tied to the plough while I'm busy on the other side of the hill working through matters with Sally Kane who's looking exquisite in Givenchy. The shadow of the shepherd in the paddock below us is lengthening as the sun heads off for its destination with darkness. It's the second time I've trotted out the name Josef Grimaldi and the second time Sally Kane has shaken her beautiful locks and replied,

'I know that name only insofar as it relates to a clown.'

I try a different tack.

'Has your husband ever mentioned a person called Josef? Or told you that he's acting as someone's minder?'

'No.'

'Does he seem even more nervous than usual?'

'N-No.'

Sally Kane's hiding something, and it's not just her legs.

'Look, lady,' I say, experiencing a feeling close to exasperation, call it edginess, 'you hired me to check out your Benedict. Well, I've checked him out and it seems like he's Simon Pure. That fact alone should make you delirious but instead you're acting like you got a heartful of iron filings.'

Sally Kane takes a deep breath.

'But we still don't know . . .'

'You're right, we still don't know turnips. But for my money it's like you told me about the seals – just like they're a protected species, so is Grimaldi.'

'What do you mean?'

'Have you ever heard of a thing called a witness protection program?'

When Sally Kane answers, she trots out the words fast, as though she's already thought out her answer long ago but doesn't want me to know she has.

'Isn't that when – someone gives evidence that – how would you phrase it – puts someone away – and because of that evidence – other persons are out to – want to – get them – that is, punish them for giving that evidence?'

Couldn't have put it better myself.

'And you think this person Grimaldi –'

I nod, but something doesn't add up and I don't like things not adding up.

'By my reckoning, this Grimaldi gave evidence that got two nasties put away. As a result, Grimaldi was placed in a witness protection program.

After that, the two nasties escaped from lawful custody and now they're after Grimaldi.'

'And you think that David's minding this Grimaldi . . .'

Edith Burton bears all the hallmarks of a government agent and by my reckoning David Jones has been reporting to her.

'It would account for all the guns.'

'All what guns?'

I tell her about the gun in David Jones's left-hand drawer as well as the rifle in his office.

That's when Sally Kane starts to look guilty.

'Oh, poor David,' she says. 'So shouldn't we – drop the investigation?'

There's just the right degree of hesitation.

I think about the murder of a singing teacher, the killing of the singing teacher's soi-disant lover, Little Miss Twisty, the potshot someone took at Rory, plus what I strongly suspect was the near abduction and murder of my daughter, Imogene.

Not to mention the thumb.

'It's too late for that,' I say.

'What if I suspend payment?'

The sun's setting, the sheep are in the home paddock and the shepherd's shutting the gate on them but that's still no guarantee against the foxes.

I shake my head.

'Sorry, lady, but this caper's gone way beyond payment.'

From the direction of the wombat farm I make out the sound of a motor starting.

I say my goodbyes to Madam Kane and get myself back to the farm, fast. But I'm too late: the hoods have freed themselves and they and the cabriolet are no longer in residence.

I don't need Aunt Rube to tell me you need two thumbs to tie number eight wire.

Nor that the hooks that Handsfree wore on the end of his arms might make a very effective pair of boltcutters.

Chapter 36

THE CORPSE ON THE CHAISE LONGUE

Early next morning, having ridden the last train back to Sydney, caught the bus, walked the walk, rowed the dinghy, run the engine to charge the batteries in order to get the pump going again, had a few drinks and caught up on the beauty sleep, I shave, using the bailing bucket, the Dettol and the straight edge, rebandage the thumb, check my remaining teeth, drain my sixth coffee for the day, and feel more or less human again.

Then one of the cellophanes rings – the one with the wild African throb to it – and it's Sunday, so I get down to the bilge fast before someone gets it into their head to complain there's some gypsy living on a boat in the harbour, with nothing better to do than drag down the value of very expensive harbourside real estate.

'Rainbow?'

'Depends who's asking.'

It's what you say when you don't know who's on the other end of the phone, or who might be listening, before giving them something worth listening to.

'I'm sorry to bother you on a Sunday.' It's the Dwarf. 'But I couldn't raise Rory.'

If it's Sunday, Rory is down on his knees somewhere begging forgiveness, and he won't be getting up for anyone, unless that Someone happens to be God.

'I've obtained the information you requested. Two persons arrived from America at about the time you mentioned and went to the address given –'

'Not on the phone.'

'The usual place?'

There's urgency in his tone.

'The usual place.'

'Good' – the urgency changes to relief and relief to anxiety – 'as soon as you can make it.'

The usual place is closed owing to sex objects not being big sellers on Sundays. There's a sign in the window taped to the portside breast of a blow-up doll between a pink suspender belt and a pair of blue velvet handcuffs saying RING MY BELL. I do like it says and a dusty rattle echoes among the dildos, instruments of flagellation and sado-rags. While I'm waiting for a response I turn my back to the door and cast my peepers up and down the Boulevard of Broken Dreams.

I work my way back through the dialogue.

I got here as soon as I could but I've got a feeling that as soon as I could might not have been soon enough.

The door's got a Lockwood, a back-to-base alarm and a slide bolt weighted down with a double-thud Yale but there's no striker for the Lockwood and the door jamb's made of maple, meaning it turns into splinters under a nudge from the deltoid. A back kick en passant to the little black box via one of my whitesides disables the alarm.

The gat finds its way into my fist as I make for the back of the shop where the stairs are.

Nothing moves, not even the Lifelike Model with Edible Mammaries next to the DVD rack featuring post-Christmas specials, including the ever-popular *Naked Santa on Ice* and *The Orgy of the Christmas-Tree Fairies*.

The periodicals carry the usual quota of flesh but the stairs at the back of the shop feature nothing but yesterday's echoes.

I set the whitesides to Mute and start climbing.

Christianity's closed.

I could stay on the top step and wait to get myself thrown back down by whoever's in residence or I could get myself into the Dwarf's office fast.

I get myself into the Dwarf's office fast.

I dive as I enter, hitting the floorboards in the roll-ready position, what's left of the thumb tucked under me, gat held with the elbow in the 'L' shape of the quick shooter. I do a triple-loop with half-spin that takes me away from the window and towards the chaise longue, ending in a forward crouch by the bookcase at the foot of the recliner featuring a deluxe edition of *The Encyclopaedia Brutannica*.

There's still silence.

I hunch out of the crouch.

Then I stand out of it.

The swivel chair's vacant and no one's holding the broken cup adorning the Persian rug on the floorboards.

I turn to the chaise longue.

It's upholstered in white, there's a dame on it, she's naked as the day, and she's a looker.

Make that *was* a looker.

I place her age at time of decease in the vicinity of thirty-five.

She possesses cornflower blue eyes, a retroussé nose, ruby red lips, hair of a colour that all the available evidence suggests is original, and a shif sticking out of her chest at about the region where the heart should be.

Death's not a good look on anyone, least of all a beautiful blonde.

I shelve the gat.

The office clock says thirty minuets after noon.

I glance around the room.

There's still no one in it.

I turn my eyes back to the dame.

She's still dead.

I use the Dwarf's phone to call Rory and tell him to organise a house clean.

Then I ring the Dwarf.

He's short.

'Where are you?'
'The usual place.'
'I've just come from the usual place.'
'Where are you now?'
'The other usual place.'

There aren't that many joints you can get drugs on a Sunday and par consequence the boofs and sidlers and pants boys and ultraspans have flocked to O'Leary's like pigeons to the crone that dishes out day-old bread at the Fountain.

Hank the Barman sidles up on the other side of the counter wearing a natty little purple one-piece with *Suck Me* on one breast and a flower on the fob, doing a job of work on a decanter that looks like it's already done a couple of rounds with the Dishlex.

'Looking for the Dwarf, Rainbow?'

I adjust the fedora, grass-green with a metallic glow to the check but minus the feather – you attract less attention if you dress down – and chuck a glance around the hooch-parlour.

It's the usual crowd, and the pianola's empty.

'Something freaked him out. He said you'd find him on the Strip.'

When I finally locate the Dwarf, I also discover that he's edgy.

He keeps flicking his eyes about him as we hoof it along Macleay, surrounded by flaneurs acting like they're in Paris, and that anyone apart from them cares.

'Someone planted that corpse on me.'

'It's been taken care of.'

'That's not the point. The point is: why would anyone plant a corpse on me?'

'Pal, you had Prisons and after that you had Immigration. First you're locking people in and after that you're locking them out. It's not a situation that's going to win you friends.'

'Plus I'm a dwarf.' He goes all subdued on me. 'But even all that doesn't add up to a corpse. It's because I'm doing this job for you, right?'

'Probably wrong. What have you got for me?'

The Dwarf glances behind him again before bringing his peepers back to mine.

'I got a couple of names, but they're neither David nor Jones.'

He runs his fingers through his orange hair.

'Go on.'

'Every person that enters this country is required to fill out a yellow card, which is then handed to Customs upon disembarkation.'

'They'd be those little cards they hand out to distract you from the perils of landing and afterwards chuck in the shredder?'

The Dwarf shakes his head.

'They're not just to distract you and they're not shredded. They're assessed, filed, and the details are entered into a central computer.'

'Okay,' I tell him, 'so you tracked back ten annees like I asked you to and Edith Burton's name pops up on two of these little cards.'

'Seven years ago, to be precise.'

'And the reason Edith Burton's name pops up on two of these little cards is that two jokers intended staying with Edith Burton after disembarkation, right?'

'Wrong.'

'What do you mean, *wrong*?'

'They weren't jokers, they were dames.'

I don't like dealing with dwarfs, never have.

'Let's get this straight. You're telling me there were two dames, and both of them stayed with Edith Burton?'

'Like I told you, the cards are cross-referenced and –'

'What were their names?'

Name numero uno: Sarah J. Churchill.

'Description?'

He turns smug.

It's a little-known fact, he tells me, that with security the way it is these days – due to the threat of terrorism and the effect that acts of terrorism can have upon share prices – airlines no longer content themselves with what people tell them. They get out there and do some research of their own.

'Tall, plain, olive complexion.'

'And the other hoop-la?'

'Josephine Turner.'

'Description?'

'Blonde, little turned-up nose, and going by the description, a peach.'

The corpse on the chaise longue.

'Who we discovered subsequently moved to a second address.'

'One she went to after staying at Chez Burton?'

The Dwarf nods.

'So feed me the second address.'

The Dwarf tells me: 221B Baker Street, Craydon.

It still doesn't add up.

Two dames arrive in Australia, followed seven long years later by the hoods.

After which one dame decides to turn herself into a corpse.

Knowing the hoods, it doesn't take much to work out who killed her.

Now all I've got to discover is:

The dame's connection to the hoods;

The hoods' connection to David Jones; and

David Jones's connection to Grimaldi.

I return my attention to the Dwarf.

'I need you to check out two more arrivals. They're recent and –'

The Dwarf shakes his head.

'Sorry but I've just finished repaying any debt I had to Rory.'

'I'll need the prints back.'

'You know where to find them.'

The call to Rory takes less than a minute.

'Your pal the Dwarf just ditched us. We need a fix on an American dame, name of Josephine Turner.' I tell him the details. 'Your friend the Dwarf will supply you with the prints.'

'Willco.'

Rory did his apprenticeship in the army.

Chapter 37

THE LAST WORD

The mailbox at 221B Baker Street is overflowing, the washing's got dust on it and the lawn hasn't been vacuumed for a week.

I lift a Harvey Norman brochure out of the box, let myself in via the green ColorBond gate and make my way down the side path like I own the joint, the Taurus waltzing in three-four time against my pectorals.

I stuff the shooter down my schnauzers, take out the laundry louvres, stack them on top of a pile of dog droppings, place the jacket on top of the glass, stand on the jacket, and heave myself up through the aperture.

Drum-beats are hammering in the missing thumb, but I'm healing, and after I land in the laundry, I'm still healing.

Whoever was here last fully intended returning, otherwise there wouldn't be a Kentucky Fried extra-large rotting on the kitchen bench next to a sheet of paper with a corner torn out of it. I also wouldn't be holding my nose with the hand not holding the gun, the one that's still got the thumb on it, as I step over the stain on the kitchen linoleum and into the room where they kennel the television.

From the opening gambit I can see this is no permanent habitat, because the relevant issue of the *TV Times* isn't sitting on the lounge with programs rough-circled in blue, a pair of slip-ons isn't lying abandoned on the carpet, and there's no half-empty mug on the coffee table, with Pall Mall cigarette butts floating in the dregs, and lipstick marks on the cigarette butts.

In fact, there's nothing but a green Smith's alarm clock

lying face-up on the rug, with the hands behind the little glass porthole freeze-framed at twelve.

The joint's got all the hallmarks of what's known in the trade as a staging post, a fly-by where jokers water the horses, pay a visit to the john, grab a kip and find themselves a schooner of chips and a warm beer before scampering back through the postillion to the stagecoach, and there's no one standing on the stoop to wave them goodbye.

It's like no one ever lived here, and even the dust's been dry-cleaned.

It tells me something, but it's to the tune of the gate clicking, followed by the sound of footsteps advancing along the footway, and I decide to make myself scarce before someone else decides it for me.

A cop – it's got to be a cop – is trying out the doorbell.

I'm back in the company of the chicken when I hear the wood in the front door splintering.

You got to do things in this business you'd never do in front of your mother.

The fowl next to the paper with the corner torn out of it tries to slide onto the floor as I shove a fist up its gizzards, putting my other mitt where the beak used to be in order to stop the thing slithering to the floor.

Hoofbeats are sounding in the hall, and it's a short hall.

A Rent-a-Crowd of maggots is doing a tango over the paper as I drag it out of the lucky-dip.

It looks blank.

I pocket it anyway, and am just leaving by the back door when the first of the hoods snow-boards in on the maggots.

While the paper's getting warmed by the blow-dry powered by the *Wooden No*'s auxiliary, I get the main engine up and running and spend an hour working the pump. The bilge is starting to look like your average suburban swimming pool.

After that, but only after that, with the bilge happily spewing effluvium, I dust the paper with the grey powder and take a visual of the prints, matching them against the ones on a piece of the daisy-patterned china salvaged from the Dwarf's. They come up positive.

I then get to work with cotton wool soaked in a Condy's crystals and methylated spirits solution and eventually a bit of writing appears, in a nice shade of yellow-brown. It's a bit like the stain on the linoleum floor, the blood that should have been on the chaise longue but wasn't, the address on the piece of paper the Dwarf palmed me, the address that, going by the advertising material and the chicken, hasn't been lived in for a week, and the body carted off post-mortem to the Dwarf's, to add to the illusion that that was where the crime took place, in order to put the frighteners on the Dwarf.

Which means the corpse that used to be the living Josephine Turner but ended up dead on the chaise longue wasn't a random killing but a specially-selected and premeditated murder. Whoever killed the travelling companion of Sarah J. Churchill knew where Turner was and for what purpose she happened to be there as well as what to do with her after she turned into a corpse.

Someone needed to kill the dame.

That same party also wanted to put the frighteners on the Dwarf.

They decided to do two jobs in one.

And whoever they were believed that after they killed Turner they would be in the clear, that no one could trace them to the deed.

But in her last moments, the dame worked out not only who was coming for her but also what was in their minds while they were on their way.

That was why she wrote what she did on the bit of paper and why she stuffed it in the chicken, in the hope that, while her killer-to-be wouldn't be any the wiser, someone like me – or an accomplice like Sarah J. Churchill or the Burton dame – someone with the know how to search for a clue anyway, would find it.

The writing on the scrap of paper is scrawled like it was written in a hurry, without much concern for the slope of the characters or their shape, the way someone would write when her murderers were halfway up the hall, and it was a short hall, and she guessed one thing – apart from the identity of the killers – and that was that she was no more than a couple of hot breaths away from becoming a corpse.

The letters aren't all that clear but I can be sure of the last two, and they suggest the first.

This is how it reads:

Chapter 38

THE DEATH OF A FED

It doesn't make sense.

The dame had five seconds before getting bumped off and she uses them all up writing a word that means peanuts.

Doesn't make . . .

But there's no future sweating over a word that doesn't make sense.

I got to find myself something that does.

We're in a coffee joint at Bondi with the surf swelling and jokers around us with a lot of time on their hands. Clint's still Clint, he's still got the gormless expression on his face, he still looks guilty as hell, he still acts like he understands the meaning of life, and he also still looks like he doesn't.

The difference is that he no longer has a job, because the broad that gave him the list also gave him the sack after discovering good old Clint, everyone's mate, busy boffing somebody else.

'So I can't do what you're asking me to do, mate.'

'You got the numbers David Jones contacted. All I want now is the same thing in reverse.'

'Yeah, but –'

'If you can't do it,' I tell him, 'you can back-pay the price of your kids' education, not to mention what you owe me for all the humiliation and defeat.'

Clint bends his attention to his skinny latte.

'Mate, that's blackmail.'

I shrug.

'If you feel happier putting a name to it, that's as good a name as any. But whatever you call it, I want a list of the numbers the Burton dame called and you're the joker that's doing it.'

'You're not looking all that well, Rainbow,' Aunt Rube says. 'Are you sure you're getting plenty of protein?'

Rube likes to keep up with my protein intake.

There's been some sort of preliminary hearing and it's gone well so they've taken her out of solitary and we're out in the exercise yard, well out of reach of the prison's listening devices, but the cameras are still rolling and they've still relieved me of my pintos, belt and fedora.

'Yeah.'

Rube nods.

'The dames still treating you bad?'

'That's what I want to talk to you about.'

'Is it Pandora?'

I tell her it's not Pandora.

Pandora's been quiet of late.

She mostly is when I'm busy.

'So tell me,' she says.

So I tell her, especially about the word Josephine Turner wrote on the bit of paper and stuffed in the chicken. When I've finished, Rube gets me to describe the dames I'm talking about, including the corpse, and she listens intently all the while, the way Aunt Rube does, and after I've finished she's silent for two laps of the exercise yard, after which she's no longer silent.

'I been thinking, Rainbow. This word "Red" – was there any punctuation? A full-stop or something?'

'Nothing.'

'Let me see it.'

I palm her the paper and she shoves it in her kick without looking at it.

'Let's try another tack. What if this Chinchilla –'

'Churchill.'

'– and the Burton broad were one and the same?'

That puts me on Pause.

Rube has always been able to put me on Pause.

'How would that help us?'

'For a start, it would explain why the Churchill dame no longer exists.'

There's a commotion at the far end of the play pen but I pay no attention, on account of Rube's still talking, and when Rube's still talking I listen.

'Even though a name was given on the little immigration card, it doesn't mean the person existed, does it? So why shouldn't Sarah J. Churchill have simply become the person she was staying with?'

'Edith Burton?'

'You got it in one.'

'Hey, you!'

The screw puffs up like a loaded alibi.

'You the dude gave his name as Grey?'

The questionnaire will take its usual course.

'Depends who's asking.'

'I said, is Grey your real name?'

'As real as it'll ever get.'

'Have you got another one?'

'Close friends call me Fatty.'

That gets me back to Reception, as well as a black eye, my belt, shoes and fedora.

My mind's still swimming with ideas of what RED might mean long after I get back to the boat, check over the engine, catch a few hours' sleep, row myself ashore, call Rory from a public phone, and bus-it to the place where we agreed to meet.

Aunt Rube's given me something to think about.

Rory provides me with something more.

It's not yet dawn, with moonlight glistening on the airline billboards, as I crunch across the frosted foliage to the place where Rory's waiting, shivering in the early morning cold.

'Is the kid okay?'

Rory nods.

'I haven't seen the dame for a while. Apart from which I scored some intelligence.' Rory means that strictly in the sense of information. 'Tex owed me one.'

Everyone owes someone, it's what makes the world go round.

'Who's Tex?'

Tex turns out to be a Pittsburgh, US of A, housebreaker whose acquaintance Rory made during a little stay on suspicion of murder in a New South Wales correctional centre – make that prison – where Tex was residing while waiting to be sent back to wherever he came from.

'He's back in America where he got himself a job in Security, and I asked him to check out the names the Dwarf provided, and regarding Josephine Turner he came up with pure gold.'

We find a cab and I tell the guy the station.

'So what did he come up with?'

'He got a mate in the Bureau to check out the prints of Josephine Turner.'

The prints on the cup from the Dwarf's, the prints of the blonde that wound up dead on the chaise longue.

'Bureau?' There's only one Bureau that I've heard of, but I've got to be sure. 'You mean the United States Federal Bureau of Investigation?'

'That's right, the good old FB of I.'

'And?'

'The swab came up positive.'

'This dame's fingertips were on the FBI's records?'
Rory nods.
'You're dead right they were.'
'On account of she was a major malfeasant?'
The nod turns into a shake.
'So what was she, if she wasn't a major malfeasant?'
'She was an agent for the FBI.'

Chapter 39

THE MAN WITH THE STRAW-COLOURED HAIR

It's early morning and I've got a train to catch but Rory's still talking.

I'm only half-listening.

Seven years ago US Federal Agent Josephine Turner flew herself into Sydney airport in the company of a second female – one Sarah J. Churchill – both giving the address where they'd be staying as that of Edith Burton.

At some point, Agent Turner moved out of Edith Burton's address and into the staging-post.

Where she lived on and off for several years – doing whatever it is that FBI agents do – until the hoods arrived on her doorstep and she was killed, joining what is turning out to be a very long string of corpses.

And all I've got is a word she wrote on a bit of paper and some joker's name, Grimaldi.

RED . . .

Short for Redhead?

In which case maybe the Dwarf killed her.

Or RED meaning Blood.

But why would a woman about to die bother writing Red meaning Blood?

'Do you know anything else about her?'

'She thought she was always right.'

I put the conundrum to one side and come back to the other problem.

'Okay, that covers Sarah J. Churchill. But what about Grimaldi?'

I find it hard to keep the urgency out of my voice, because something in the back of my mind has just made its way to the front of it, and that something is very scary indeed.

Rory shuffles his foot.

'Tex didn't want to say, because he reckons any debt he owes me isn't worth dying in the repayment of.'

'Why should he die?'

'He says that's what happens to people that mess about with Grimaldi.'

Which tells me something about Grimaldi.

Only I need to know something more.

'Can you get the Dwarf back on side?'

Rory shrugs.

'I'll try.'

'Okay, we got the name Grimaldi and it's coupled with the name of someone from the FBI. Now I want you to get Dwarfie to match the two names with Legal Action, US of A.

'I think we're closing in on the reason why the hoods are after David Jones.'

The train's an express so it's a few minutes after eleven as I climb out at Dashiell, discover from the timetable at the station that the last train out will be at five, and make my way along Main Street.

The sweat's working up a lot of enthusiasm under the shoulder holster as I near the ruins that pose as the local infirmary.

At three pounds fully loaded, the Smith & Wesson 686 is the heaviest item in my luggage rack.

The lightest is the stethoscope I picked up at the apothecary's in Main Street that I sling around my neck as I elbow my way through the swing doors of Dashiell Base Hospital and hoof-it along the corridor of Building numero uno, nodding to a cleaner in mauve pyjamas as I pass.

The odd nurse glances in my direction but I make like I'm a visiting doctor and they give me the benefit of uncertainty.

Accordingly, I'm making satisfactory progress until I get to Coronary, where I discover the flaxen-haired shepherd emerging from a door with *ANGUS MACIVER, M.D. M. Surg. F.R.C.S. Reparative Surgeon* neatly engraved upon the wall beside it.

The joker's wearing a suit and somehow he's got himself into the wrong paddock entirely but he's still wearing the thatch of straw-coloured hair and that's how I recognise him.

I also recognise danger when I see it and that's how I find myself shoving open a door and backing into a little room as the joker turns. I cop a profile that I've seen before, not only in the company of a bunch of sheep and at a distance, but also sitting slurping caffeine in close-up, as well as in several other locales.

I don't do coincidence.

Coincidence produces a lot more questions than it answers, and among the questions are:

Why has this joker been watching me and Sally Kane?

And what is he doing here now, posing as a doctor?

I've got the door half-closed and there's no way the joker can see me but I've caught a glimpse of the sort of all-seeing eyes you only find on the very guilty, and their owner's standing stock-still, like he's feeling my presence rather than seeing it and he's busy reaching out with his nerve ends to locate me.

I go into freeze frame, like when Rube would stop one of her movies to explain a Cagney dance step or what it was that Bogart was up to when the cops found him or how the P.I. worked out that the match-seller was a killer, and the shadowy images flickered on the dining-room wall, guns blazed, bodies sprawled all over the shop, and hoods kept the motors of their De Sotos turning over in the sunshine until the lesson was firmly implanted in my cerebral cortex, at which point Rube would remove her hand from the drive-spool and allow the movie to continue.

I count the seconds and there are five of them but it seems like an eternity before Blondie starts moving again.

Following him would answer a lot of questions, only I'm not about to follow him because just as I start out the door a voice from behind stops me.

'We'll have to stop meeting like this.'

I turn.

Even though she's seated on a Fowlerware and her trousers are down around her ankles, Sally Kane's still as poised as ever, like she's just had a patient's head shaved and she's about to start in on a trepan.

'To what do I owe the pleasure?'

I turn away and address the door.

'I thought something might have happened to you.'

'It has' – the voice is still cool – 'I've discovered I can no longer rely on my privacy.'

Chapter 40

THE LADY IS A LIAR

Sally Kane's fully dressed and she's mooching about her office. The office is a cubicle with cracks in the walls and boards on bricks for bookcases and the books might look dishevelled but the red nose I gave her all those aeons ago looks very nice sitting next to the telephone. This is situated next to the biro-and-pad set that every doctor likes to have beside them for writing their death sentences on.

I'm in the swivel chair behind the desk.

I lean forward.

It exposes the gat but I leave the coat open anyway.

'Isn't it about time you levelled with me?'

The colour drains from Sally Kane's face quicker than water comes into the *Wooden No* when the pump fails.

'I – I have been – levelling with you.'

'Lady,' I say, and it's like we've come full circle, 'you haven't levelled with me since the moment we first met.'

The sounds of the infirmary grind on around us, someone coughing their last, the beat of witch doctors' bongos, and a hospital cleaner motoring around in the hall just outside the office with a vacuum.

At this stage in the questioning people have got two options.

They can go on lying.

Or they can confess.

Sally Kane does neither.

'I – was worried that you mightn't take on the case if I – told you everything.'

'So now you can be worried I won't stay on the case if you don't.'

Sally Kane drops into the chair that's normally occupied by

the patient, and her voice drops to a whisper.

'The day we first met I – I was desperate.'

The Hoover's still hoovering and at any moment someone could bust down the door and let rip with a carbine.

I don't close the coat.

'I didn't know where else to turn.'

Sally Kane reaches out and picks up the red nose like it's a lifebuoy.

'All right, the truth is I – wanted a divorce from David because I – no longer loved him.'

'So you were lying when you told me you wanted to have his baby?'

'Yes,' Sally Kane whispers.

'Did you know anything about his history?'

'I – already told you. No.'

'I know what you already told me, lady, that's why I'm asking again. Did you know anything about his history?'

Sally Kane sucks in a lungful of hospital air.

'All right, yes, yes, I did! At least I – I guessed.'

Her voice is raised.

I like it when they raise their voice.

It means there's a chance they might be telling you the truth.

'You live with someone and there are hints, giveaways,' she goes on, 'and after that there are more hints and more giveaways until you end up putting together a profile.'

'A kind of patient dossier?'

Sally Kane nods.

'So how does this particular patient dossier read? The one you put together on David Jones.'

Sit someone in the right chair and they become what the chair says they are.

Sally Kane has become the patient.

She takes a deep breath before she continues.

'Look, I know paranoid as a word is unscientific,' she says, shifting in the chair that's normally occupied by the patient, 'at least it is the way people use it today. But using the word unscientifically, David shows all the signs of being paranoid.'

'Thinks jokers are following him, reading his thoughts, spiking his tea, out to kill him, and so forth?'

'Yes.'

'Why might that be?'

'Because there might be a good reason for someone to follow him.'

'So why didn't you tell me this in the first place?'

'Because I – wanted a second opinion. And I – didn't want to colour your judgment. Also I – was afraid you mightn't take on the job.'

A lot of reasons.

On a countback, too many.

'What about you?'

'What do you mean?'

'Is someone watching you, too?'

She reddens.

'No. All right, I mean yes.'

'Who?'

Pause.

'I – don't know.'

I try another approach.

'What makes you think you're fine and dandy when you say that someone's following you when the same thing on your husband makes him paranoid?'

Sally Kane sits up straight and takes another one of her deep breaths.

'Mr Scutt, you once asked if it was a woman's intuition that made me think something might be wrong with David, and I replied, No, it was an informed judgment.'

I remember.

'Well, I'm beginning to think intuition is nothing to be ashamed of.'

I've got one more question so I ask it.

'Does the word Red mean anything to you?'

Just then the telephone rings.

Sally Kane puts down the nose and answers it.

I look at the chronometer.

It reads just after midday.

Chapter 41

THE MAN IN THE MAUVE PYJAMAS

'Sally Kane here.'

Dr Kane's all business as she bends her pearly to the business end of the receiver.

'Name?' She's got the biro in her hand and she's busy writing on the pad with it. 'How soon you can get her to the hospital?'

She makes with the Yeses, Noes, and Maybes, particularly the Maybes, before jamming the receiver back in its bassinet and responding to the unasked question I put to her.

'A car was forced off the road adjacent to the Dashiell abattoir, hitting the slaughterhouse at such speed that it smashed through the double-brick wall just above the offal chute. The driver was hurled the length of the killing room floor and onto a meat hook.'

Sally Kane's standing, no longer the patient, no longer even patient.

'Serious head injuries ensued, requiring immediate surgery. I'm sorry but I have to go.'

I get a feeling.

Call it intuition.

'Who was it on the meat hook?'

Sally Kane bends to the pad.

'The name on the licence read – Edith Burton.'

She pauses in her headlong rush to the door.

'Wasn't that –?'

Her pause enables me to get to the door before her.

I grab the handle, wrench it open and discover the joker with the Hoover down on his hands and knees. And he isn't dusting.

'Look, I really must go!'

Sally Kane's already said that. There's no reason for her to be between me and the joker on the floor, because the patient must still be all of twenty minutes away.

The parabellum's already in my fist and the words are already forming in my icebox.

'Hey, you!'

It's what you say when you want to grab hold of someone but can't because a dame's between you and the joker who's been listening at the keyhole, a joker who might be all dressed up in cleaner's pyjamas – cap, mask and gown – but is no cleaner than he ought to be, and who even now is hurtling past Reception and headed for the door marked ESCAPE.

I park the gat and turn back to where I last saw Sally Kane.

'Isn't that the joker who –?'

But Sally Kane's no longer there.

Lesson No. 103: faced with a choice between two pursuits, choose the one least likely to succeed.

In the light of Lesson 103 this is a no-brainer.

I know who Sally Kane is and where she'll be when I want her but I don't know anything about the joker in the mauve pyjamas except that I strongly suspect he can help me with my inquiries.

Chapter 42

DEATH BY FIREBALL

A codger in a wheelchair finds himself sprawled on the floor as I charge down the corridor after the cleaner. At least the codger's in the right place – a nurse is already helping him to his feet and stitching him back into the wheelchair.

Meanwhile, a figure crawls out of a broom cupboard wearing nothing but long johns.

I leave via the swing doors.

All I can see in the hospital grounds is sunshine.

I swivel on the path and pound my way towards the carpark.

An ancient green Toyota Coronary is at the boom gate and a mauve-pyjama'd arm is carding the auto-go.

I take three-point-five seconds over the hotwire of the early-model Mazda in the Nurses' lot, point-five seconds to lever the transmission onto the small cog, do a three-pointer, and launch the crate across the paddock as Mr Pyjama guns the Coronary southwards.

The thing about booms is they bust easy.

An alarm sounds as I rip past the sentry box, splintering the boom, and keeps right on sounding, a *whoah-whoah* that follows me according to the law of diminishing returns as I hammer the heap down Hospital Drive, left past the showground and around by the Christian Girls' Brainwashing Establishment, before swivelling right up the hill towards the racetrack.

The Toyota's drawing away.

Early-model Mazdas might be easy to break into but they're nobody's number one choice for a chase. Mr Pyjama's already past the guards and halfway up Nimrod Straight while the 121's still smacking the brains out of its pistons in Camshaft Canyon.

It's Sunday so something must be happening on Mount Goodyear and the something that's happening is a veterans' rally in celebration of the town's sesquicentenary. The crowd thinks we're in it as Mr Pyjama guns his jalopy into the first turn hard on the heels of the tailenders, while I spin past the Guadeloupes at the barrier before starting in on the long grunt up Heartbreak Hill after him.

Your average punter loves death and nowhere outside a warzone is death more imminent than on a racetrack.

I'd put the crowd at ten grand and the starters at around the fifty-mark as the chequered flag waves us into the next lap, the two of us screaming into contention for line honours, even though neither of us is even entered in the race.

I hug the rails as a 1947 Buick Vee-Eight full of chromework and curves and superiority nudges the Toyota into the outfield.

The joker at the wheel of the Coronary might be able to handle a Hoover but he can't drive a car for pecans. As he comes into corner numero quattro, I note he's gone out too wide and his tyres are squealing so I paddle back to midstream as he throws out the anchors in a desperate attempt to correct the slide. This has an effect totally contrary to the one he was after.

The mob howls as Mr Mauve's rear end flicks around, putting him amongst the ads for spark plugs and beer and a holiday in Hawaii, scraping his portside fender as he goes into a wobble, and potential dingle or not, I go in after him.

I need to head him off, come up on the outer edge and go into a slide on his portside on the way out. The crowd sees the rescue coming, or better still, the possibility of bloodshed, and is on its feet and screaming for injury, but above all death.

It's then that I notice the cabriolet.

It's still black and it's still upright, it's ahead of the Coronary and it's enough to distract me from my good intentions. I slam on the sizzlers when I should be accelerating and the outside donuts to drag when they should be wheeler-dealing and the Mazda to flip, taking out an FJ, an XL, a PR, an APC and a couple of Plymouth Brethren on the way.

The somersault takes me over the ring board, I enter a planetary system unsuspected by your average astronomer, and there's not much left of anything by the time I come out of it. Thankfully there's more of me than there is of the Mazda, which appears to have been cobbled together out of no more than blind faith and goosebumps.

I locate what remains of my senses, decant the shooter and smash the dregs out of the windscreen. I then drag myself out of the car past the registration sticker, the wildlife pass and the next service reminder. The paramedics scurry my way with their little black bags and red tape and clipboards full of good intentions, so I dust down the Gatsby jacket and melt into the crowd.

The cabriolet's still burbling around the racetrack – I can see it wavering as it wobbles into Hell's Corner – but the Toyota's gone into retirement in Hawaii. The other crates are veering to avoid it as it lies on its back in the dust, wheels turning in the air, smoke elbowing its way out of the engine, and low-octane spilling down from the gas tank to join it, like lovers too long parted.

I can't handle fire.

Not after what happened to my mother.

Not after what happened to my sister.

Not after what almost happened to me.

The blond is a Rorschach blot against the driver's-side window, the sort of shape psychiatrists come up with using bits of paper and a splat of Waterman's ink, imperfectly symmetrical, with what might be fingers spread against the glass like a salamander's. The fingers are framing a central blob that could be an upside-down head or a heart or a lump of coal or a piece of faecal matter. Whatever it is, it's being pressed in place by the bulge of the airbag, inflated when the vehicle smacked into the circuit board, tea leaves on the inside of bone china, foretelling a hangman's future.

The blond joker's features have come into sharp relief and

real fear is etched in his pale eyes. I can see the man's past like I'm doing his dying for him – a figure in the caff where I first met Sally Kane, a shepherd beside a cottage by a hillside, a doctor in the hospital, a cleaner kneeling outside Sally Kane's office door, and now a just-about-to-be-dead man at the wheel of an upside-down Coronary.

Unlike David Jones, the blond joker's got a lot of past.

What he hasn't got is a future.

The blast when the smoke says hello to the petrol reverberates around the mountainside and sends a burial shroud of smoke into the air. It also hurls me back up the hill whence I came. When I open my fire-scarred eyes, the blond joker's still there, only he's no longer blond, his fingers are no longer fingers and his face no longer has any features in it.

Flames are licking the sheen off the duco, the tyres are sizzling and the airbag's deflated, leaving what remains of the shepherd to sag against the Toyota's window like a fire-struck Lepidoptera that flew too close to the candelabrum.

The rest of the cars are still hurtling around the track and among them is the black cabriolet, dancing by on its third or fourth or fifth or sixth runabout. The passenger-side window is down and Babyface is leaning out of it, hard eyes scanning the scene like he wouldn't mind having been responsible for the wipe-out, as well as any other deaths that might be going.

I half-expect the business end of a machine-gun to appear cheek-by-jowl with the cherubic face and start filling the air full of sunshine.

Chapter 43

OPERATION DEATH

At 3.15 pm by her office chronometer, Sally Kane's got blood on her hands, and that makes two of us.

She shouldn't have, because surgeons wear gloves when they're surging, but there must have been a hole in her Ansell's or else she sliced them while she was gouging around in Edith Burton's brain pan digging out the bone scraps that had knifed their way into her cerebellum when she went through the windscreen at the abattoir.

And I shouldn't have, either, except that my past got in the way of me saving the shepherd.

I've rebuckled the holster, reblocked the fedora, dusted off the denims, and patted down the flapdoodles on the jacket's storage system. I've also put one and one together and come up with angst, so I'm not in the mood to pussyfoot around with anyone. I shove my way past the gurney with the green sheet over it outside Sally Kane's office and barge in without waiting to be invited.

Sally Kane looks like she needs treatment.

Accordingly, I apply the electrodes.

'Your boyfriend's dead.'

She turns porcelain.

'I don't have a boyfriend.'

She's right.

She doesn't.

Not any more.

'Dead and cremated,' I tell her, 'so you can stop pretending you were going to all those meetings to save the hospital, when in reality you were rendezvousing with your lover.'

I give that time to sink in.

'You can also start helping me with my inquiries.'

If her face were any whiter it would be risotto.

'Wh – what happened?'

I tell her what happened and I don't spare her feelings in the telling.

She falls apart, and it's a long time before she falls together again – the little nose wipe comes into play, the sobs are real sobs, and for once the emotion is genuine.

I give her thirty seconds, because that's all I've got.

'I once asked if you knew anything about the word RED.'

Sally Kane shakes her head.

'All right, then I need to see Edith Burton.'

She takes one of her deep breaths.

'I'm sorry,' she replies, 'but Edith Burton was involved in a serious accident. It was touch and go but I believe we got to her in time. I've inserted a steel plate in her head, she's in a serious but stable condition, and if she's allowed good and sufficient rest she's got an excellent chance of making a complete recovery.'

Enough clichés to paper over most of the problems in the public health system.

'It just so happens that I can't allow her to rest on account of I need to interview her,' I say, 'and I need to interview her fast, and to do that I require a room number.'

'I'm afraid that's not possible.'

'Then neither is your staying alive.'

'Wh – what do you mean?'

They always want to know what you mean, even when they already know. I've got nothing to lose by telling her.

'The jokers that are after your husband have now bumped off everyone connected with him except you.

So – apart from your husband – you're the last man standing.'

'How do you know?'

They always want to know how you know, even when they already know. I tell her anyway, and at the end of the telling, Sally Kane's ready to agree to anything.

Edith Burton's in Room 327B, she tells me, at which point something starts squeaking on the other side of the door, and it isn't rodents.

'But I warn you,' Sally Kane says as I make for the hatchway, 'she mightn't make much sense. I've seen a number of such cases, and I know that such trauma can manifest itself in confusion.'

It's a chance I'm prepared to take.

Because now I'm prepared to take anything.

Chapter 44

A BULLET FOR BURTON

Intensive care units are like morgues.

The difference is that in morgues the corpses have stopped breathing.

The gurney with the green sheet over it looks familiar but I've got no time for familiarity as I hotfoot it up the hallway to Room 327C. I press the EMERGENCY button beside the bed, waiting behind the door until all available hospital staff have answered the call before slipping out, letting myself into Room 327B, and easing the door shut behind me.

Edith Burton is lying on the bed but she's no longer Edith Burton.

Instead she's a figure in a waxworks, a bundle of machinery humming around her, a mask over her face, wires attached to chest, arms and legs, and tubes coming out of her nostrils. There's a lot of dried blood, her head is swathed in bandages and there's a fearful look in her eyes that grows ever more fearful as I remove the mask from her face and seat myself on the visitor's chair beside her.

'If I don't return this,' I say, holding up the mask, 'you're going to cark it.'

'What do you mean?'

'Expire, cease to exist, extirpate, pass away, perish, die.'

It wasn't what she asked but it's what I'm telling her.

'I mean . . .'

'I know what you mean, lady, but what's important right now is what *I* mean and right now I need to know who you are.'

She shakes her head.

'Okay, play it the hard way – what's your relationship to David Jones?'

Again the head shake.

Maybe she's trying to clear it.

Or maybe she just wants to die.

'Why are the two hoods after David Jones?'

The front door to her transigence is locked, so I try the rear entrance.

'Tell me about the accident.'

She must be dead keen to get the mask back on because she tells me about the accident, but in the telling of it her voice is the rustle of a bloodstained gown on a sickroom floor and I can only just make out enough to understand half of what she's saying.

And half of what she's saying is that she was accelerating around Abattoir Bend on her way to Dashiell when a car appeared out of nowhere, forcing her vehicle across the road and into a stone fence and through the brick wall of the slaughterhouse.

But I already know that.

'Why were you coming to Dashiell?'

She stops to draw breath.

It's a long breath and there's a lot of blood in it.

Meanwhile, one of her mitts is creeping towards a button that looks very much like the one I pressed next door.

I make to chuck the mask across the room and Burton withdraws the hand from the button, fast.

'Now tell me who was driving the car.'

Burton shakes her head, which suggests either that she didn't see who was driving the car, she can't say, or she just doesn't want to live. Take your pick.

I hear the door behind me opening but I continue with my line of inquiry.

'Colour of car, year of manufacture, marque. Was it by any chance a black cabriolet?'

Edith Burton's not answering.

'Josephine Turner, then. Your fellow FBI agent. Tell me about her.'

'Disappeared . . . don't know what . . . happened to her . . . Arrogant bitch . . . liked to be able to say she could . . . work things out before . . . anyone else could . . . Can imagine her on . . . her deathbed . . . saying . . . I told you so . . .'

Quite a speech, only I'm not interested in speeches.

'What does RED mean?'

Edith Burton looks confused.

Also she's suddenly looking very afraid so I figure I need to forget the car and Josephine Turner and head back to the garage.

'Grimaldi, then. Who's Grimaldi?'

Edith Burton opens her mouth only it's not to speak.

Her head's turned my way and her eyes have still got fear in them only they're no longer focused on me but on a point just behind me. When I see that, I immediately bring the interview to a close. I drop the mask and go for the gat, at the same time moving into a high-danger spin, the sort of movement that needs no flex-for-weight-transference and is therefore more or less directionless, but has the advantage of giving no warning of your intentions.

I manage to bring the drip feed down around my lugs as I go but I've effectively taken myself out of the line of fire so that when the shooter goes off and the bullet hole appears in the middle of Burton's bandaged forehead, I don't know if the bullet was meant for me or for Burton or for both of us. What I do know is that the mask won't be helping her any more, because her condition has suddenly deteriorated and a recovery of any sort is out of the question – complete or otherwise.

I swing my peepers in the direction of the door, disentangle myself from the drip feed, kick away the chair and dive back to the bedside, in order to catch whatever it is that Burton might have for me, in the way of last words.

'Gurgle,' she says, eyes rolling.

I check the damage and discover that the reason Madam Burton didn't die pronto was that the steel plate Sally Kane inserted in her head deflected the slug.

The bullet's still found its way into her brain.

And she's still saying Gurgle.

But she's also trying to say something else.

It sounds like 'cycle path'.

But why would anyone worry about cycle paths when they're just about to be dead?

Chapter 45

THE DEATH OF THE DWARF

Aside from the gurney – its green sheet trailing on the chessboard floor and whoever was under it gone – the hallway's deserted, with nothing to kick up a breeze in it but the doors.

I hurl myself down the passageway, gat at the ready.

A doctor, three nurses, the tea lady and a cleaner emerge from Room 327C, see me and demerge back in to it.

An attendant gets in the way, then gets the hell out of it.

An old dame with difficulty walking sees me, and suddenly has no trouble walking at all.

Screams come from a room on my right.

I slam open the door, crouch between the architraves, and brace myself in the knees-bent, legs-apart position, gun gripped in both fists at the ready.

A dame's lying on her back in pretty much the same position, and when she catches sight of me she stops screaming.

Maternity would be a lot quieter if they called in the assassins.

I shelve the gat and start back to where I left Sally Kane. I've still got some unanswered questions as well as the odd unquestioned answer and Sally Kane is now in very serious trouble indeed.

As I reach the weed-strewn lawn the last joker I expect to see is David Jones, but that's who I see.

He's strolling from the direction of the visitors' carpark whistling Dixie. He's moving with short, quick steps in the direction of the hospital.

He doesn't look my way as he pushes through the doors.

He's on his way to see Sally Kane which means she'll be back under his protection, and that frees me up for other duties. I reach for one of the dead-men's mobiles and en route to the station dial C for Clint.

'I need those telephone records.'

'Nearly there, mate, but –'

I tell him to get completely there and where I'll be in a four-hour train ride from now so he can hand me the results. He hasn't quite completed his side of the dialogue.

'I think I'm being followed.'

What is it with people?

'Look, pal, everyone's being followed, it's called traffic, just be there.'

I thumb the red button and phone Rory as I hoof it past all the sesquicentennial celebratory signs lining Main Street. I make it into a carriage just as the dame in the railway uniform flags away the riff-raff on the platform and the doors close.

It's just after nine in the pm when I reach Sydney Central. Rory's waiting on platform numero uno, and so is the latest obituary.

The Dwarf's dead, Rory tells me, but not before the little man managed to file away a stack of documentation about the size of a Patrick White novella. This is what Rory's got in the faded canvas dilly bag over his shoulder.

'Why aren't you watching Imogene?'

'I can't be everywhere, Rain!'

I shake my head and head off up the concourse.

Stations make me nervous.

So does Rory.

'Tell me what happened to the Dwarf.'

The Dwarf considered the devil and the deep blue azure and Scylla and Charibdis and a rock and a hard place and the frying pan and the fire and et cetera and so forth and finally came down on the side of incaution. This resulted in a bunch of papers being heisted from a courtroom in America.

Just after the Dwarf took delivery of the papers – but not before he'd safely parked them with Rory – he was standing at the window of his office when some person or persons unknown waltzed in and shot him.

I interrupt Rory's discourse.

'How do you know all this?'

'The porn merchant told me.'

'The porn merchant told you and you believed him? Did the porn merchant even see who did it?'

Rory shifts his foot.

'Well, he was at the Dwarf's when they came for the little man but he dropped behind the desk as they entered. He heard the shots, came out of hiding after they left, saw the row of bullet holes on both sides of the window and the Dwarf slumped on the floor beneath them, and cleared out. I found him downing hotshots at the hooch parlour – that's when he told me.'

Some things have to be taken at face value and among the things I have to take at face value are Rory, the porn merchant, and the death of the Dwarf.

No more than half a block away, I hear a car engine burble and die, a car door slam and the sound of hurrying footsteps.

A couple of beats.

Then the same again, like an echo.

Another dying engine, another car door, more footsteps.

I keep walking while next to me Rory keeps crutching.

It's getting dark as we head up Alum.

'Hang onto that bag,' I tell Rory.

'Where are we going?'

'We're meeting someone.' That's when I hear something. 'Shuddup!'

Someone's following us.

The list of suspects has shortened.

The shepherd and the Dwarf and Burton are dead.

Which just leaves the hoods.

I indicate east, and at the same instant head in the other direction, grabbing the fedora as I go and ending up in a crouch while the gat comes out for an airing.

The footsteps stop.

The world's reduced to a blob of light on a deserted footpath – courtesy of a single bulb lamppost – and a bunch of shadows.

I stay where I am.

Rory stays where he is.

The tail doesn't move.

The world stops on its axis.

The trick to moving quiet, Rube taught me, is the same as any other act of camouflage – imitate your surroundings.

So I imitate my surroundings.

And my surroundings are a Vinnies donations bin surrounded by sacks of donations, a lot of darkness and an office building possessed of faulty air-conditioning.

I do the air-conditioning.

It's no more than a muted clunk and whisper but that's what I do, picking up the sound and lifting it a notch or two, using my diaphragm like Ruby taught me and producing a continuous clunk and whisper that covers the shuffling of my feet as I move through the undergrowth that in this part of the world passes for landscaping.

The tail's standing by a bush.

I spot him because he's not imitating his surroundings.

His outline's fuzzy.

Rory's nowhere to be seen.

Lesson number one when you discover you're being tailed: assume the opposition's sharper than you are. You'll never be disappointed.

Lesson two: assume that patience in these situations isn't a virtue. It's a necessity.

And lesson three: assume nothing.

Chapter 46

THE END OF THE LINESMAN

At last count, there's half-a-dozen deaths, leaving eight lives remaining in my care, eight people to keep in the land of the living – Imogene and the twins; their mother; Sally Kane and David Jones; Rory; and last of all, Clint, who we're now on our way to keep a rendezvous with.

Whoever's out there is the enemy. I can't hear the enemy breathing but I can see it, great chunks of carbon dioxide metabolising whitely in the cold night air.

Lesson four: always let your follower make the first move because the first move will always be the wrong one.

The follower steps into the light.

That's when I recognise him and that's when he gets shot, hands flying up to his chest, body thrusting forward in an off-centre half-turn pirouette, legs crossing, followed by a free-fall, a pitching-forward and simultaneous crumbling so that all that's left at the end of all the fancy footwork is a ragged pile of clothes on the footpath, like just another donation to Vinnies.

Lesson five: stay where you are.

I stay where I am.

That's when another person steps out of the darkness.

Correction: another *two* persons.

The hoods.

Handsfree is carrying a gat and the gat's carrying a silencer.

He kicks the sack so it rolls over.

'He's dead.'

Babyface shakes his head, but it's not in wonder.

'No kidding.'

'I was just saying.'

'Yeah, well don't just be saying nothing, it's enough that you exxed the bastard.'

'Well, he was hand-in-glove with that Rainbow banana, wasn't he? Him and the cripple? Ain't that why we're following him? Ain't that why he was with them?'

'He wasn't with them, you ape, he was in process of keeping a rendezvous with them.' Babyface peers into the darkness, his baby face glossy in the half-light. 'And because you were so bloody trigger happy, we lost them.'

They're still dressed in black and they still haven't got a brain between them.

While Babyface goes through Clint's pockets, Handsfree stands over him with the Stechkin.

Babyface comes up with what have to be Burton's telephone records and shuffles to a spot under the light where he frowns over them.

Rory motions me to shoot them both and I motion him to stop motioning.

'Just a bunch of telephone numbers,' Babyface says to no one in particular. 'No names, just telephone numbers.' He stares at the paper. 'Except one's got a circle around it.'

He looks up, and under the one-bulber I can see inspiration on his baby features.

'So what do we do now?'

'We find out where this number is and we pay it a little visit.'

After they've gone, Rory crawls out of the woodwork.

'Why didn't you pin him?'

A killer doesn't break the habits of a lifetime overnight.

'Life's not just about pinning people, Roarer.'

'So what do we do now?'

'We get ourselves back to Dashiell, fast. But first we got to rid ourselves of a corpse.'

I don't hear the hoods' vehicle departing but that doesn't mean rhubarb.

We find a black garbage bag among the donations to Vinnies and wrap Clint in it.

After that, we get ourselves a taxi cab, one of those big ones that people cart wheelchairs about in, and get the corpse, ourselves, and Rory's dilly bag into it.

'Where you taking the garbage?'

I tell the cab-jockey the harbour.

Chapter 47

DESPERATELY
SEEKING SAFETY

The harbour's a fine and lonely place.

At night, lights glimmer on its surface, the sound of ferry klaxons carry clearly across the inky water and corpses are weighted down and dumped in places where only the sharks can find them.

When we get to the rocks where the tinnies are I tell the cab-jockey to wait.

The depositing of bodies in the harbour requires a sound working knowledge of seabed geography and also tides and eddies, as well as a chain plus a large rock to tie the body to in order to stop it making like a soufflé and rising.

'It's a small boat,' Rory observes as we manhandle Clint into the coracle. 'It'll sink under our combined weight.'

'It won't sink under our combined weight because our weight won't be combining.' I get the boat into the water. 'Me and Clint are going for a little boat ride while you're taking the cab back to town and collecting the Caddie. And don't forget the dilly bag.'

I row to a spot just past Point Hopeless where I dump Clint.

There's no eulogy.

The black water closes over his body like he never was and I row back to shore that much easier for his passing.

We're in the Caddie.

Rory's at the wheel, we got the dog between us – the one with the big head, Little Miss Twisty's pooch, the dandie Dinmont – and there's not much in the Caddie in the way of armoury.

'Where are your tools of trade?' I ask Rory.

'I gave them away. But I still got the crutch. Where we heading?'

'Swing by the kid's.'

'What kid's?'

'My kid's, the one you're supposed to be protecting. But first, you can chuck me one of your phones.'

I ring the jail.

'Any further thoughts on that word, Rube? We're going in, and –'

'As a matter of fact, yeah.' Rube's voice is hollow, like she's talking from a death chamber. 'Remember we were talking about acronyms? Well, I –'

But the connection drops out. I check the little window. It says, OUT OF CREDIT.

'Anything the matter?' asks Rory.

'Yeah.' I chuck the dead phone onto the back seat. 'We're not moving.'

Salina answers the door and Imogene's beside her.

At least one of them looks surprised.

'What are you doing here?'

'I'm taking the kid.'

'Over my dead body you are.'

Once upon a time we used to love each other.

Now all we got in common is the language, and Imogene.

'Her life's in danger,' I say.

Salina sighs.

'All right. But if she goes, I go with her.'

I climb in the back seat with the kid and the pooch while Rory sits behind the steering wheel glaring at Salina.

'What's she doing here?'

'She's the mother.'

Rory thumps the wheel.

'I know she's the mother. What I'm asking is what she's doing here.'

Too many questions, too little time to answer.

'We're taking them to safety.'

'Where are you taking us to, Daddy?'

'Safety.'

Even as I speak, just up the street I think I see a shadow.

Maybe it's Pandora, maybe it's the hoods, or maybe it's just a shadow.

But I got enough on my plate without worrying about shadows.

Chapter 48

THE MOMENT OF TRUTH

Imogene picks up on what she thinks I told her.

'Are you taking me to see my sister?'

People hear what they want to hear.

I shake my head.

'I said safety, not Sophie.'

'So when can I meet Sophie?'

I'm heading for a confrontation, only I didn't know it would be this kind of confrontation.

I like stand-ups, two men, two guns, kind of thing, I don't do subtle.

'Look, she's not where we're going, okay?'

'She's never anywhere we're going. Why can't I even meet her, if she's my sister?'

Sophie's been a great comfort to me over the years and I don't want to give her up but I don't want to risk losing Imogene, either.

'She's –'

My throat's seized.

The Caddie's rocking into the night, and if the two up front are talking, I can't hear them.

'She's what, Daddy?'

Salina cranes around.

'I'm sorry but did I hear right? You've got another kid besides Imogene?'

She doesn't add and the twins.

Instead she turns on Imogene.

'And you knew this but never told me?'

Imogene shrugs.

'Daddy told me not to say. He said it was our little secret.'

'Have you ever spoken to this sister you've never seen?'

Imogene turns away and stares out the window.

'I can explain,' I tell her.

But Salina explains for me.

'What Daddy's trying to say,' she tells Imogene, 'is that this so-called sister of yours doesn't exist. There's no Sophie, because – for reasons best known to himself – your father made her up out of his head.'

There's a lot of silence after that.

Imogene finally turns towards me.

There's more than just the dog between us.

'Is that right, Daddy, what Mummy just said?'

It's the moment of disillusionment, when the kid finally discovers her daddy's a fruitcake.

'Is what right?'

'What Mummy just said about my sister.'

I look at Rory's neck but there's no inspiration there, just a lot of dirt and a bullet hole, and Salina's staring through her side of the split windscreen.

'There's no Sophie?' Imogene's eyes are shining, and it's not with an excess of love for her paterfamilias either. 'And there never has been?'

I shake my head and nod it all at the same time, on account of Imogene's asking two questions and the answers to the two questions are totally different.

'There was a Sophie,' I say, when I finally manage to get the words out, 'only she wasn't your sister.'

Imogene frowns.

'Whose sister was she, then?'

I take a deep breath and when I do there's dust in it.

'Mine.'

Chapter 49

DEATH BY WINDMILL

Salina turns in her seat.

'Let's play Colours, shall we?'

'What's Colours?'

Come midnight there aren't all that many vehicles on the road and what there are aren't all that easy to see but somehow the game grows legs and pretty soon everyone's got a colour and forget they're locked in the car with a loony and are yelling, There's one! and Is that blue?, even Rory.

That's when I see it.

Imogene's won two out of three and I haven't been doing all that good but that's only because I keep getting dealt the wrong colour, when Imogene chooses blue, Rory's on red and Salina's got yellow, while Imogene's lucked white and I've been landed with the colour nobody wants, if you can call black a colour.

'Red!' yells Rory.

'That's not red. It's red and blue.'

'And yellow.'

'And white.'

I look where they're looking and where they're looking is at a B-double circus truck which accounts for all the colours, with pictures of ringmasters and acrobats and clowns all over it, and colours all over the clowns.

'That counts as one for everyone except Daddy.'

'That's not a car,' I tell her. 'It's a truck.'

'It still counts. And there's one for you, anyway.'

That's when I look in the looking glass and that's when I see it, dancing from lane to lane and having no trouble at all keeping up with the Caddie. It's souped-up just like the hoods said it was and its straight-up-and-down windscreen gives nothing away but reflections. It's the colour of death and just as welcoming: an upright coffin on wheels waiting for the next customer, all shined up and with somewhere to go.

I know why it's following us.

The hoods didn't depart after they killed Clint but waited around and followed us instead. They figured that our destination and the address of the phone number they pick-pocketed from Clint might be one and the same.

They're following us for the same reason that Fate follows anyone – because we've got a rendezvous.

We pass another circus truck only to find there's a string of the things, like elephants attached to one another's tails. Eventually they take their place among all the other clowns on the road while the cabriolet's still sitting bolt upright behind the Caddie and I'm the only one who can see it, because the world's moved on since the Colours game, but that doesn't mean Imogene's moved on as well.

'Where's your sister now, Daddy?'

'I don't think Daddy likes talking about his sister,' her mother says, 'so let's drop the subject and all have a little nap, shall we?'

These babies are gas-guzzlers but we've done the fuel stop and while we were at the gas station we've made the necessary trip to the Damen und Herren. All of us except Rory that is, who was happy to mix it with the dog up against the ice container. This was how he came to surprise the joker in the balaclava. The pooch went ballistic and the joker only just managed to escape to his conveyance and drive off.

Now Rory's curled up in the back seat with the kid and the dog, they're all wearing seatbelts, even the dog, and snoring their heads off, leaving me up front with Salina and too many memories.

It's started to rain.

'You tend to be full of questions,' she says, peering past the wipers, 'but you're not all that free with the answers.'

She taps at the wheel, frowning.

'This crate's handling funny.'

'It's a funny crate,' I say, 'or else it's the rain.'

The night's deepening and we've had the question-and-answer dialogue and the this-crate's-handling-funny conversation but sooner or later Salina's going to get back to what's really bothering her.

'You never told me about your childhood.'

I shrug.

'It was just another childhood.'

But she's not buying what I'm selling.

'As far as I can make out your sister died when you were quite young and for some reason you feel guilty about it, so guilty that all these years later you're still pretending she's alive.'

I don't answer.

It doesn't stop Salina.

'How old were you when she died?'

I feel the automobile shift from side to side, along with my world.

'Was it an accident? Did she fall off a cliff?'

'No.'

'So how did it happen?'

I can't stall forever.

'I was five and Sophie was three. Dad was a pusher and my Mum was a hop-head. You could say it was a marriage made in Heaven.'

Salina's wrestling with the steering.

'It was the nineteen-sixties and the whole world was hippy. People with names like Mahatma and Shava carved totem poles out of gum trees, power came out of windmills, parents did drugs, and kids did the best they could, under the circumstances.

We lived on a collective farm where one of the chief entertainments was something called "Orbiting".'

Even after all these years I shudder.

Or maybe it's just the way the car's handling.

'Any time of the day or night some hop-head could strip off and start twirling a length of wood with oil-soaked rags on the end, burning like fury.

Accordingly, there was always a lot of fuel around, plus the necessary matches.'

And people drugged out of their brains.

'There happened to be a windmill on the Collective and the hippies had rigged up some sort of seat on the end of one of the vanes, with a ladder up to it, and on windy nights people would strap themselves onto it and whirl round, waving their fire sticks and making like they were an integral part of the cosmic cycle.

'That's how she did it.'

'That's how she did what?'

I stare out into the darkness.

'One night my mother decided to become a Catherine wheel and thought we kids might like to be part of the fireworks.

She got hold of Sophie but I managed to hide behind a totem pole.'

We're heading downhill.

The Caddie speeds up.

'My mother couldn't find me so she contented herself with Sophie. She had a can of kerosene and a box of Redi-Lites and the wind was up and the windmill was straining at its ropes and next thing she'd strapped herself into the seat and had Sophie in her arms and she was lighting matches and laughing.'

The memories are on a roll, just like the car.

'In my five-year-old mind I thought the wind might blow the fire out but of course it did just the opposite. I thought I saw a figure by the windmill but it wasn't doing anything about it so I ran out from behind the totem pole and started climbing the stepladder beside the windmill. There was a lot of smoke but I kept on climbing and when I got close to my sister I reached out to grab her.'

I have to stop for a moment.

'But all I got was her shoe.'

Salina stares out into the darkness.

'No wonder you're messed up, Rainbow,' she says.

That's when the car goes into freefall, veering towards the edge of the precipice.

Chapter 50

A FREE RIDE

We smack into a vacant rock and spin around.

There's the stench of burning rubber and the shriek of buckling Caddie.

I find myself grateful for the invention of seatbelts and the solidity of big old American cars.

Half of us is dangling in space.

The other half wants to join it.

Behind us drivers are reining in their horses.

In front of us, brake lights flash.

Something white rips past us, heading hell for leather for Dashiell.

A truck looms out of the darkness, at the last minute its lights veer around us, there's the sound of people screaming, and a horn starts a one-sided conversation with the sky.

Tyres screech.

More horns blare.

Headlights play a kaleidoscopic cacophony among the trees.

A ricocheting wheel smacks into the Caddie.

The Caddie teeters.

And through all the smoke and the stench and the racket and the ricocheting wheels I hear the voice of Imogene, saying, 'Is this the safety you were talking about, Daddy?'

I reach over, grab the kid, fling open the door and roll us out into the mud.

I catch a glimpse of the dog and the others following.

Meanwhile, figures are slipping and sliding towards us from the truck ahead, the beams of their torchlights glistening on the wet road in between.

Voices in the maelstrom.

'Give her here!' Salina drags the kid out of my arms. 'Bloody Rory's bloody heap wouldn't handle, it was like trying to steer a Dodgem, the bloody brakes failed.'

Rory takes it personal.

'There was nothing wrong with the brakes, she just got the million-mile service.'

Salina shakes her head, glares at Rory and hugs Imogene.

'The brakes were useless, Rory. Ditto the steering.'

The figures from the truck have reached us.

'You lot okay?'

'Our car's stuffed. We need a ride.'

'We're going to Dashiell.'

'So are we. Chuck us a torch, will you?'

I motion the others to go ahead while I make my way back with the torch.

Steering doesn't just go, brakes don't suddenly fail and cars don't suddenly head for the nearest cliff, not even when they're eighty-year-old Caddies.

I lie on my back in the mud and shine the illuminator up under the chassis.

The steering's of the Gemmer-worm-and-Sector kind.

I don't know how it got into a Caddie but I know why it's no longer operative – the pump line's gone walkabout, while the rest of the system is pretzels.

I don't need to check the brakes, but I do it anyway.

In these crates, brakes require actuating rods.

But the Caddie's brakes have been de-actuated.

Someone's cut them.

I slide out from under.

The road looks like a landslide.

There's the sound of sirens, actuated by fifty or so mobile phones calling Emergency.

I don't want to be here when the cops come.

I make for the truck.

'Tell me about the rubber-necker.'

'What rubber-necker?'

We're squashed in the cabin of the truck, the truck's on its way past a quagmire of traffic trying to go the other way, and Rory's frowning.

'The one at the servo,' I tell him, 'the joker in the balaclava, the one you found checking out the Caddie, the one Rocket went ballistic over.'

'It wasn't a joker.'

'What do you mean, it wasn't a joker?'

'It was a dame.'

Chapter 51

LIFE IS A CAROUSEL

We're almost at our destination before the guy at the wheel breaks his silence.

'Time for you lot to get out.'

'Why?'

'Because this is our turn-off.'

I blink into the night.

I can just make out a sign.

It's the turn-off to the farm.

I make a decision.

'It's our turn-off, too.'

We're back at the farm. Because it's rained, the dust is no longer dust but mud. Although the place is as dark as a murderer's thoughts, I can still see the farm's no longer a farm but a circus, complete with Big Top and sideshows and a generator roaring in the front paddock and a crane rearing up into the night sky and arc lights picking out the shadows of workmen as they busy themselves setting up a ferris wheel.

'Where are we?' Salina asks.

'It used to be a farm.' The No. 8 wire's still there, with the loops in it where I'd tied up the hoods, along with the plough and the memories. 'It was leased to a couple of jokers that weren't farmers.'

Rory's down on his knee.

'Thou art the resurrection,' he's croaking, 'the truth, and the light!'

The rest of us slosh through the mud to the shack.

By the light of the torch I make out the black patches on the roof and a note on Jones, Jones and Jones letterhead attached to the door with the sort of tacks generals use in world wars while they're standing around converted billiard tables wondering what battalion to sacrifice next, complete with little red tips on them to indicate the progress of the enemy:

TO WHOM IT MAY CONCERN

Due to a lease being broken and as Dashiell Council considers it ideal for the purpose we have leased this farm to the circus.

Cottage still available For Lease. Inquiries . . .

'Hey, you!'

I spin around, torch in one hand, equaliser in the other.

The torch picks out a joker coming our way, squinting into the beam.

I lower the torch and shelve the gat.

'What's your game?'

I make it up as I go along.

'We're renting the house,' I tell him, 'what's yours?'

The joker jerks his head over his shoulder to indicate shapes of tents in the darkness and the crane swinging a steel section into place for the ferris wheel.

'I'm the circus.' He squints harder. 'Look, I'm sorry but I get nervous because we've got a lot of valuable equipment here and our security people have been held up en route.'

The crane swivels in the early-morning darkness behind him.

'There was an accident in the Mountains – some idiot nearly went off a cliff and the cops have closed the road while they investigate. Meanwhile we're supposed to be in the parade so I thought seeing you're here you might keep an eye on things and in return your kid can have a free ticket to the circus and a ride on the ferris wheel.'

I tell him yeah.

Tell people yeah and they get out of your way.

Mr Circus's hoofs gloop in the mud as he moves off and he's

got to shout over his shoulder to be heard over the racket of the generator.

'You can pick up your free ticket at the booth, just tell them Pete sent you.'

After a while, the circus people drive off, leaving nothing behind but the Big Top, the sideshows, a few spare vehicles, and the ferris wheel.

The car approaches from the direction of Dashiell, pausing briefly at the gate before coming on again, a white car travelling out of an incipient sunrise along a dusty, weed-strewn track between straggling eucalypts next to the paddock in which stands the carousel, its skeleton sharp-etched against the sky, and its empty seats dangling.

Chapter 52

THE FIGURE IN THE BALACLAVA

The person climbing out of the Commodore's familiar.

I like familiarity.

It breeds contempt.

The kid, Salina, Rory and the dog have got themselves into the shack while I'm out front toting the Husqvarna, which to seamstresses spells sewing machine, but to me means gun.

The figure trudges through the mud towards me.

I store the gun and meet her halfway.

'Why, Mr Brown!' It's Goggle Eyes, the receptionist from the realtor's. 'So you decided to take the place, after all!'

I tell her yeah.

'Oh, goodie!' She claps her hands but after that looks warily about her. 'Look, I'm sorry we haven't cleaned up after the last tenants but they left in something of a hurry and it's so hard to find cleaners when you want them and they were behind in the rent and really we all felt so let down they seemed so nice, all dressed up in their black suits and the rest of it and it was me that did the renting, Mr Jones didn't even see them, and . . .'

From the shack behind me comes the sound of barking.

But I haven't got time for dogs.

'Where's your boss?'

'You mean Mr Jones?' The dame's no longer pretending there's more than one, apart from which she also appears distracted. 'He's – disappeared.' She switches the subject. 'I'm so glad you're taking the place. There was a real nice man with green eyes and a missing leg that was interested but he –'

Behind me the barking has turned to Frenetic.

'I need to find him.'

'The man with green eyes?'

'No, your boss, David Jones.'

'I've told you,' she tells me again, 'I don't know where he is.'

Behind me, the shack has suddenly gone quiet.

The dame glances over my shoulder before looking back at me.

'Is there anything else you need?' She seems in a hurry to get out of there all of a sudden, feet shifting in the mud, goggle eyes shifting in her head. 'I mean, anything apart from Mr Jones, that is?'

I tell her no.

She turns to go.

'You can sign the lease when you're in town,' she calls over her shoulder.

I watch her make her way back to the car.

Even from where I'm standing, I can see the dent in the fender.

She climbs in, starts the engine, lets out the clutch, turns and motors slowly up the driveway, the sight of her progress masked by the trees, stopping at the gate for what seems a long time before starting the engine again and continuing down the road and away.

I turn back to the shack.

It's as silent as the grave.

Houses shouldn't be silent as graves.

Not when they've got a kid and a dog in them.

Despite the cold I suddenly break out in a sweat.

The Husqvarna finds its way back into my fist and I break into a gallop.

My brain's been on vacation.

It's time I called it back to the workplace.

I smash in the fly-screen, enter on the half-roll and note as I climb to my feet why the house has gone silent.

There's no kid in it.

Neither is there a dog.

Rory's not in attendance either.

In fact, the only person still in the joint is Salina and she's trussed up in the same chair I was trussed up in when I donated my thumb to it, but she's gagged with a tea towel and she's struggling.

I untie the gag.

'Where's Imogene?'

'She took her.'

'Who took her?'

'The woman in the balaclava.'

I rip off the ropes.

'What woman in what balaclava?'

But Salina's already out of her chair and running.

There's a back door and she's out of it and she's screaming.

That's when I get out after her and that's when I see what she's screaming about.

There's no sign of Imogene and all that's left of Rory is a crumpled heap and the crutch by the tank.

At least he's moving.

Next to him lies the pooch.

It isn't.

I swing back to Salina.

'Give it to me from the top.'

So she gives it to me from the top and from the top Salina and Rory were inspecting the hut when the dog started barking like mad out the back, after which the dog stopped barking like mad, and Imogene burst in on the run.

'There's a woman here!' she screamed.

But it's all she manages to get out because the next thing they know a dame wearing a balaclava appears behind the kid with a rifle in one hand and Imogene in the other. Imogene stops running and starts crying instead.

The dame's waving the rifle.

Rory's been around enough murders to know when he's in the middle of one so he does what's required without the dame having to say a word, trussing up Salina while holding the dog under one arm and the crutch under the other before obeying the beckoning of the firearm and accompanying the kid and the dame outside.

Rory's coming to.

I turn my attention to him.

'What happened?'

When Rory shakes his head, drops of blood fly out of it.

'The dame told me to jettison the pooch, after which she whacks it with the butt end of the rifle before whacking me over the head, and decamping with the kid.'

'Since when couldn't you handle a dame?'

'She had the drop on me and she was a big dame.'

'Where's Imogene?'

'I told you. The broad took her.'

'Describe the broad.'

'I told you, she was big.'

I give him the cut-glass chandelier look.

'That's all you got for me, she was big?'

'She had this balaclava over her head, for Chrissakes, how can you describe someone you can't even see?'

Rory doesn't know anything else and he still doesn't know anything else as we get ourselves out of the shack, grab one of the circus cars from where it's parked near the Big Top, and head off back up the drive.

Salina's at the wheel.

'Where are we going?'

'To the land floggers. Fast.'

Chapter 53

LAST CALL

There's a sign in the window of Jones, Jones and Jones, and the sign reads VACANT.

I don't believe in signs.

I kick down the door.

The paperweight with the fairies in it is no longer on the counter and the joint smells of dust and criminal intent.

I hit Last Call on the Alexander Graham Bell and after that punch Call Back but the phone rings out into silence and tells me nothing I didn't already know.

I hoof it down the corridor to Jones's room.

That's where I find the paperweight.

Only as well as fairies it's now got blood on it and sprawled beside it is the girl, her goggle eyes shut tight and a patch of blood busy turning black on the back of her head.

I sling her over one shoulder and I'm just lugging her past Reception when the Alexander Graham Bell on the counter rings.

I reach out with the free mitt and pick up the receiver.

I don't speak.

Never answer a phone, let it answer you.

Sometimes it does, sometimes it doesn't, and sometimes it tries to sell you a holiday in Majorca.

This one does.

'Is that you, Mr Scutt?'

Only one person calls me that.

I give a grunt in the affirmative.

'I'm sorry but I missed your call. I'm ringing about our appointment.'

There was no appointment but I give another grunt in the affirmative.

'Remember we were to meet at twelve?'

I grunt again.

'Instead of twelve, can we make it one?'

I wasn't supposed to meet anyone at twelve.

I shift Goggle Eyes across to the other shoulder.

'Is Imogene with you?'

'Yes.'

'Remind me where we're supposed to be meeting.'

'The usual place.'

The phone goes dead.

I look at my chronometer.

It's going on for eleven-fifteen.

The usual place, Sally Kane tells me.

At one, she tells me.

Not twelve, but one.

I got to rely on nothing happening to Imogene in the meantime.

I carry Goggle Eyes out to the car.

'Is this another one of your little popsies?' asks Salina.

I ignore the commentary and park the dame in back of the wheels with Rory.

I've got to save Imogene.

But first I've got to see those papers, the ones Rory's got in his dilly bag.

'Hand me the papers.'

'What papers?'

'The papers I told you to get, the ones your pal Tex lifted, the court papers from the US, the ones in the dilly bag, the bag I told you to keep your eye on.'

'It's in the Caddie.'

And the Caddie could be anywhere.

I check my timepiece.

Five minutes have passed.

'We're nowhere without those papers.' I think for a moment. 'Give me the numberplate of the Caddie.'

Rory gives me the numberplate of the Caddie.

'Now a driver's licence number.'

Rory gives me a driver's licence number.

I get myself back into the realtor's.

The joint still smells of dust and criminal intent, the PC's still on screensaver, the nasturtiums could still do with a makeover, and the phone connects me to the cops.

'I'm the owner of a Caddie,' I tell them, 'and I want it back.'

'Name.'

'I just want the Caddie.'

'Name.'

I tell them Rory's name.

'Licence number.'

I tell them the licence number Rory gave me.

'Registration number of vehicle.'

Three minutes.

I tell them the registration number of vehicle.

The three minutes turns into seven.

Then, 'I'm sorry but that vehicle is the subject of a police investigation.'

'What investigation?'

'It was involved in an incident.'

'Where is it now?'

'That's not for me to say. First, you got to present yourself at Dashiell police station.' Suspicion enters the voice; suspicion always enters the voice. 'Were you the driver at the time of the incident?'

'The car was stolen.'

'Are you saying it was stolen at the time of the incident?'

'That's exactly what I'm saying. Look, I just need something out of it, and it's urgent.'

'Then all you got to do is present yourself at the station.'

I haven't got time to present myself at the station.

Present myself at the station and I can kiss the rest of the day goodbye.

I haven't got time to kiss the rest of the day goodbye.

Because it would also mean kissing goodbye to Imogene.

Madame Kane's got my kid, she's telling me to come and get her, I've only got until one in the post-meridian to do it, the answer to how I'm going to do it is in Rory's dilly bag, Rory's dilly bag's in the Caddie, and the Caddie's –

The cop shop's on the other side of Dashiell. They're clearing Main Street for the parade and accordingly we pass a lot of vehicles clogging up side roads and congregating in paddocks and cops manning the barricades and a long while after that we find ourselves at the cop shop.

From where I'm sitting I can see a building with a big blue-and-white sign on it saying POLICE. Poking out from behind it is a tall, pink tail-fin that could only belong to the Caddie.

Five more minutes have passed.

To go through the hoops will take more time than I got.

I tell Rory to create a diversion.

Goggle Eyes is still off in 3D land.

Rory tears himself away, slams open the door and crutches his way quickly to the cop shop.

Thirty seconds later I'm sidling around the backside of the Caddie.

I get down on my hands and knees and reach up to the door handle. It's locked.

The thing about driving with dogs is that people keep windows open just wide enough to let the stale air out, but at the same time keep the dogs in.

Just wide enough for a hand.

I reach up through the opening, unlock the door, open it, and crawl in.

The dilly bag's not immediately apparent.

I hear Rory yelling words to the effect of, Give me back my frickin' car, or else . . .! which should be enough by way of diversion.

I check the floor of the Caddie, but there's only footprints and breadcrumbs, and then up the back, where there's nothing but more breadcrumbs, a lot of mould and a noddy dog.

I reach in where the well-padded back seat fits under the well-padded backrest.

I find a sixpence dated 1927.

There's also a receipt from the Hillbilly Church, thanking Rory for the cash donation.

There's also something else.

The dilly bag.

I grab it, get myself out of the Caddie, ease the door shut, and head back to the wheels.

Chapter 54

THE STOLEN PAPERS

Salina's got the motor running.

Rory appears in the doorway of the cop shop and starts crutch-hopping across the concrete towards us, a covey of cops hard on his heel.

Rory can move when he wants to and right now it looks like he wants to.

I reach behind, sling open the door and Rory falls in on top of Goggle Eyes.

'Let's go!'

'Where to?'

The cops are nearly on us.

I glance at the clock on the dashboard.

Twenty-three minutes to twelve.

'Back to where we came from!' I tell Salina. 'The other side of Dashiell! Go!'

Salina goes.

I flick through the papers.

The name of the court's been blacked out and so have most of the names, but behind all the legal malarkey and the dead hand of judicial censorship, the facts are still there.

And the facts are that ten years ago, in a well-to-do suburb of Chicago in the US of A, one Josef Grimaldi was hacked to death at his place of residence in an attack of unprecedented savagery.

While Salina hammers the vehicle in the direction of Dashiell, I read on.

Grimaldi initially worked for the Mob – for Mob read Mafia – but subsequently turned informer.

And a few months into blabbing to the Federal Bureau of Investigation all he knew about the Mob, he suddenly finds himself dead.

But Grimaldi's fifteen-year-old son – hereinafter referred to as XB1 – happened to be at home at the time of the crime, running downstairs when he heard his father's screams over the noise of the radiogram, to discover his papa all chopped up in little pieces on the floor in the company of two men he happened to recognise, the taller of whom was waving a meat cleaver.

But – and this had to be one plucky little potato – while the hoods were standing around admiring their handiwork, the kid snatches away the cleaver and gets in a couple of good swings, forcing the perpetrators to flee, one of them minus his hands. The kid's left grieving over the remains of his father, which is the position in which a neighbour, alerted by all the excitement, found him.

The handless hood was arrested when he presented himself to be doctored at a nearby infirmary.

It wasn't hard locating his fellow assassin.

The kid did the ID on them and the two hoods were charged with Grimaldi's murder.

The legal procedure took a few years but the kid's evidence finally nailed the perpetrators.

The kid was subsequently placed under a witness-protection program to ensure that his fate didn't follow that of his father.

There's a hand-written addendum and like all good addenda it's brief.

Witness XB1, who has been equipped with a new identity and relocated and is understood to have started a new life, was subsequently awarded twelve million dollars in damages, to be paid by the Federal Bureau of Investigation as compensation for the death of his father. Grimaldi Senior was considered in the employ of the FBI at the time of his demise, and the

Bureau failed in its duty to afford him adequate protection.

I look at the date of the addendum.

It's a week prior to the time Sally Kane contacted me.

About the time Sally Kane noticed David Jones to be acting even stranger than usual.

It's like tumblers falling into place when you're cracking a safe.

David Jones isn't minding a protected witness called Grimaldi.

David Jones *is* the protected witness called Grimaldi.

Josef Grimaldi Junior was hustled onto a plane to Australia disguised as a woman – namely Sarah J. Churchill – in the company of FBI agent Josephine Turner, who on arrival handed him into the care of special agent Edith Burton.

Josephine Turner then moved to a safe place – namely 221B Baker Street – from where she undertook other duties for the FBI.

Meanwhile, Josef Grimaldi Junior took lessons in voice to disguise his American accent, got plastic surgery which produced the regular features Sally Kane told me about, and then set up in Dashiell as a realtor, a business requiring the minimum of qualifications, and therefore ideally suited to a joker in hiding.

And met and married Sally Kane.

And they were all set to live happily ever after, except that four things occurred.

The surgeon that had done the work on Josef Grimaldi Junior moved to Dashiell, met Sally Kane, informed her that David Jones wasn't who she thought he was, and became the disillusioned Sally Kane's lover;

Josef Grimaldi Jr was awarded a lot of money;

The two hoods escaped and tracked Grimaldi to Australia, vowing vengeance; and

They found a private detective on the same trail they were and decided to follow him.

Which explains everything except all the deaths.

As I consider these facts, a sheet of octavo falls out of the sheaf of papers and finds its way into my mitt.

Chapter 55

THE TRUTH WILL OUT

We're nearing town, the traffic's getting heavy and we've slowed to a crawl.

It's nineteen minutes before noon.

I stare at the new bit of paper in my fist, where I make out the words DISALLOWED, INADMISSIBLE AS EVIDENCE and NOT TO BE USED IN COURT and underneath, translated by me into English:

1. The father maltreated both the child and the child's mother;

2. The mother is believed to have died as a result of such maltreatment;

3. Confused and disorientated, the child was mercilessly bullied at school;

4. The kid formed an intense hatred for his father;

5. Consequently that kid can't be trusted as far as you could kick him.

It's signed by a shrink and the observation could be about me, only it's not about me, it's about some other weirdo, and suddenly all the unexplained deaths can be explained. What can also be explained is why the hoods are after David Jones – make that Josef Grimaldi Junior – with a vengeance.

Grimaldi Junior killed his own father.

He timed the killing for when the hoods were due to turn up for their usual shakedown.

Then he framed the hoods for the job, lopping the mitts off one of them in the process.

Meaning Imogene's now on death row.

I turn my attention to the back.

Rory's telling Goggle Eyes how he got the holes in his neck in a sword fight.

'Shut up, Roarer.' I turn my attention to Goggle Eyes. 'Now tell me what happened.' I check the clock: seventeen minutes before midday. 'And keep it brief, there isn't much time.'

Goggle Eyes tears her eyes away from Rory.

'First thing this morning I was at my desk when Mr Jones came rushing past me then came out to Reception carrying something in a case that only later I realised contained a rifle.'

'Was there anything odd about his appearance?'

'He was dressed as a woman.'

'Well, of course I looked surprised but he told me that some jobs were best done dressed as a woman and he was my boss so I had to believe him. He ordered me to drive to the farm where he got out at the gate, telling me to go on ahead and keep you occupied while he tidied up.

'I did as I was told; I didn't want to appear incompetent or stupid. I didn't realise what he meant by tidy up until he met me at the gate afterwards.' The girl shudders. 'He was dragging a very frightened little girl by the hand and telling me to drive back to the office or he would "zap the kid".

'Those were his exact words, zap the kid. So again I did as I was told, this time because of what might happen to the little girl if I didn't.

'And when we got to the office, he whanged me over the head with the paperweight, and that's all I remember until –'

'Did he say where he was going?'

She shakes her head, and it's then that I hear the sirens.

There are a lot of them and they're heading our way.

I check the rear-vision.

The cops are in it.

But there's also something else.

The black car.

The hoods have picked us up on their radar.

They want Grimaldi as bad as I do.

But they've only lost a couple of hands.

I stand to lose Imogene.

Chapter 56

APPOINTMENT AT NOON

I check the clock on the dashboard.

It's going on for a quarter to twelve.

One o'clock, Sally Kane told me.

That's when I get an attack of the chills.

Because Sally Kane told me words to the effect of not twelve but one, and she told me it not once but twice.

But who said anything about twelve?

Only Sally Kane.

And the reason she said anything about anything was because someone was standing beside her, making her say it.

Adding the bit about twelve must have been her idea, which was why the call was suddenly terminated.

I haul out the papers again.

Page thirteen gives the details of the death of Josef Grimaldi Senior, including the hour of demise.

The hour of Josef Grimaldi Senior's demise was noon.

I do the recap.

Twelve noon was the time Harriet Stowe was dispatched, Agent Churchill met her end at noon, it was also the hour when the Dwarf appeared to have copped it, and little Miss Twisty ditto, as well as the time an unknown car collided with Edith Burton's at the abattoir.

They were all people who, one way or another, could have fingered David Jones as being Josef Grimaldi.

Like Sally Kane said, paranoid as a term is not all that scientific.

But it will have to do until something better comes along.

Like –

Cycle path, I thought Edith Burton said.

Try *psychopath*.

Patterns make sense of motel wallpaper, they tell you when to put money on a greyhound, and they help solve serial murders.

It's like I'm reciting my tables for Aunt Rube all over again.

Once twelve is twelve, two twelves are twenty-four, three twelves are thirty-six, four twelves are forty-eight, and five twelves are sixty.

But six twelves is mass murder.

Someone was standing beside Sally Kane at the time of that phone call, that someone could only have been David Jones, and the message he told her to pass on was to meet her at one.

But . . .

Sally Kane's one very smart dame.

Shortly after her marriage to the man of her dreams she realised he could be a nightmare.

She diagnosed him as having something seriously the matter with him.

That's why she set herself to leave him for somebody else.

That's also why she hired me, to see if I could discover the excuse she needed to rid herself of him, and also why she had her boyfriend riding shotgun, to protect her in case David Jones found out.

Sally Kane had done the diagnosis, and decided there was evidence of serious illness.

The only trouble was she diagnosed the disease as benign.

It was only later that she realised it could be malignant, and that's when she started getting her changes of heart.

But she also discovered there was a time frame.

A killing hour.

And that killing hour is noon.

Which is why she told me words to the effect of, Instead of twelve we'll have to make it one.

A band's playing, the ta-ra-ra of trumpets, the smack of drums and the evil hullabaloo of bagpipes mingling with the whoop-whoop-whoop of police-issue helicopters surveilling the parade from above.

Salina pulls up in a mess of brakes.

'The parade!' she screams. 'The parade's in the way! We can't move!'

In front of us a bunch of dancing girls is strutting their stuff, in front of them again is a brass band, marking time because the float that should be in front of the band – the one with the hospital team demonstrating for better facilities for the hospital – has got all snarled up in the process of getting out of a paddock, not going anywhere and blocking the parade's progress in the process, while we've got the cops closing in on us from behind.

'Get out,' I yell, 'we got a float to catch!'

The hospital truck's being driven by a clown, which is how he's managed to catch a corner of the truck's tray on the gate post.

I rip open the hatch.

'Get out!' I tell the clown.

I pull the clown's nearside arm and it comes off in my hands.

The sirens are all around us.

I chuck the arm back in the truck, shovel what's left of the clown onto the turf, and order Rory behind the wheel in his place.

'Move it! Move it!'

Rory moves it.

The truck's an old Leyland Hippo and normally it would be carting bulldozers but right now it's carrying an operating table. There's a bunch of doctors around the operating table, except they're not operating – they're staring wild-eyed at this bunch of desperadoes that's taking them to Hell, which wasn't their original destination, all they wanted was more money for the hospital.

The black cabriolet's almost upon us, behind them are the cops, and above them again is the chopper.

Chapter 57

AT THE TRYSTING PLACE

The black cabriolet's managed to get through, mainly because the hoods aren't all that interested in life, especially when it's other people's.

It's a rough ride for the jokers on the back while up front Goggle Eyes is nursing the spare arm in one hand and Rory in the other, Salina's tangled up in the gear sticks, and Rory's one foot's working overtime on the brake, the clutch, the accelerator and anything else he can put his foot on, as the road segues into dirt and I tell him can't he get the heap to go any faster.

'But we're here.'

We're at the gate to the circus.

The tents are up, hoop-las and sideshows have appeared in the paddock, and a kid's screaming happily on the ferris wheel, turning hugely and lazily against the sky, like it's detached itself from the Earth and is busy creating its own universe.

'What did you say?'

'I said, we're here.'

'Not here!' I have to shout to be heard over the generator, plus the truck's engine, the jokers yelling on the back of the truck, the distant-but-rapidly-approaching racket of the police-sirens and the kid screaming on the ferris-wheel. 'The next place, you idiot!'

The one around the corner, below the hill where Sally Kane and I used to meet, outside which her flaxen-haired lover pretended to be tending his flock when all the time he was watching Sally Kane. The other cottage, the lovers' trysting place where Sally Kane and her lover met when Sally Kane was pretending to be at all those meetings, the joint where Josef Grimaldi's holding Sally Kane and Imogene hostage, because that way he knows he can get me, at which time he can take us all out together.

The clock on the dashboard says twelve minutes to midday as Rory screeches to a halt next to the white car with the banged-up mudguard outside the house with the madman in it, bringing more shrieks from the passengers up the back as our sudden inertia causes them to pile into the back of the cabin.

I tell Rory to stay where he is and the other three ditto, climb down, haul out the gat, and start in on the approach.

Psychopaths like patterns.

Josef Grimaldi likes twelve.

But I like my patterns, too.

And my pattern is to arrive early, and enter by the front door.

Accordingly, I arrive early and enter by the front door.

Josef Grimaldi, also known as David Jones, is alone.

He's sitting on a bed, he's wearing black tights and a green dress. On the bed next to him is a balaclava and a Browning rifle, there's a clock on the wall behind him and something red on the floor near the door. He's got a Luger in his fist and it's pointed directly at my head.

He's smiling as he speaks.

'Drop the gun or you're dead.'

I drop the gun.

He checks his watch.

'You're a tad more than an hour early.' His accent has reverted to its native Chicagoan. 'I only just got back from my little excursion.'

'I'm still on daylight saving,' I say. 'Where's my kid, Grimaldi?'

The request doesn't register.

'They used to meet here,' he murmurs. 'They were supposed to be making money for the hospital but instead they were making – whatever it was the two of them were making.'

The clock on the wall behind him says ten minutes to midday.

'Tell me about the murders, Grimaldi.'

He considers the request, then comes to a decision.

'You'll be dead yourself soon so what does it matter?'

So he tells me.

They always tell you.

It's half the fun in being psychotic, the look on the victim's face while the killer justifies the unjustifiable, just before he kills you.

Nine minutes to go.

David Jones is no longer the easy-going realtor.

Instead he's a soft-spoken lunatic called Josef Grimaldi, with something to sell besides real estate.

His own madness.

Chapter 58
THE SELF-PITYING PSYCHOPATH

'First, I killed my father.' His voice is low, calm and reasonable; he might be talking about the weather. 'He drove my mother to suicide and bullied me. He ran a numbers racket under the protection of the Mob and the standover men were due to arrive to extract their regular payment from him.

I chose that moment to kill him, despatching him with the meat cleaver and chopping him up into lots of little pieces.

Then I waited.

He smiles.

'The standover men arrived right on time. I was in pretty good shape because of all the workouts I'd done to deal with the bullies at school, so I knew I could handle them, plus I had the meat cleaver and the advantage of surprise.

I managed to hack off the bigger one's hands before they fled.'

Eight minutes.

'Go on.'

So he goes on.

After he kills his dad, frames the hoods and obtains protection, he dresses up as a dame and calling himself Sarah J. Churchill (both Rory's and the Dwarf's description for Sarah J. Churchill was big or tall – but a medium-sized man would seem tall for a dame). He then emigrates to the Land of Oz, shacking up with his Minder, Edith Burton, while he gets his face and voice reshaped before moving to Dashiell.

Seven minutes.

'What about your other victims?'

This is his big chance, so he takes it.

'The voice coach was always going to be a problem, so I took her out early. And I would have got away with it, too, except that you started nosing around.'

The fault's always somebody else's.

'And the others?'

The expression on the killer's face remains bland.

'You could say it got to be habitual. I scored the compensation but that only brought the hoods after me, and I knew it was only a matter of time before they found me so I started covering my tracks by – well, attending to detail.'

He smiles shyly, like a kid that's scored high marks after being labelled incurably stupid.

'It also gave me – this might sound strange to you – a good excuse to go on a killing spree. I realised after I killed daddy that I – well, that I rather liked killing. Next came the old girl, the voice coach's live-in. She was on the phone to you when I killed her – after a prolonged bit of fun and games torturing her – and I would have got the dog, too, only it recognised me from the previous time and hid.'

He shrugs, it was all too easy.

'I hired the axe man to keep you away from the proposed scene of my next crime – I thought that was a neat touch – while I took out Peg Leg and your kid. Except that you twigged to it and showed up too soon.

Through Edith Burton I located and killed Special Agent Turner and dumped her on your retired public servant friend as a warning, but somehow you got onto that, too.

'So when that failed, I just walked in with my trusty rifle and shot him while he was standing by the window.'

He steadies the Luger.

'Then I forced Edith Burton's car off the road into the abattoir – don't you just love abattoirs? – but thanks to my son-of-a-bitch wife and her skill with a scalpel, Burton stayed alive and I had to finish her off as she lay blabbing her heart out to you in the hospital, just missing you in the process.'

The cops must be getting close.

'That's when I came across you in the hospital grounds,' I tell him, 'pretending to be coming from the direction of the carpark. You must have moved fast.'

He shrugs.

'I kept in training.' I remember the exercise bike at Daisy Drive. 'It had become a habit. When people want to do you harm you've got to stay fit to survive.'

He crosses one leg over the other, neatly, still holding the Luger on me, also neatly.

'But you were always one step ahead of me, Mr Private Eye. You even robbed me of the pleasure of killing Lover Boy. But I can still look forward to killing all you lot, including the hoodlums, who I believe should be here any minute, plus, of course, your peg-legged mate, who unfortunately I couldn't shoot at the farm because people would have heard the shot.

'But I finally managed to kill that goddamn dog, the one that sprang me when I was attending to the Cadillac, the dog that barked whenever I was around.'

The madman's voice stays soft but his features have turned hard.

The gun stays aimed at my sternum.

Five minutes to go.

'Everything would have been all right,' he murmurs, 'if only you hadn't shown up.'

He's overlooked all the murders.

'Sally and I could have been together forever.'

Four minutes.

Tears spring to his eyes and his knuckles whiten on the Luger.

'All those people would still be alive and I would still be with Sally.'

Psychopaths like their delusions.

It's what makes them psychopaths.

'What about your father? Wouldn't he still be dead? And wouldn't you still have killed him?'

Grimaldi's got centre stage and he's making the most of it so he's crying a little.

He doesn't wipe his eyes.

He wants me to see the tears before he kills me.

But I've still got two questions before the big one.

'What was it with Beethoven? And why the obsession with twelve?'

I know the answer but I need to keep him talking.

I can hear the sound of approaching sirens.

'My father had *Song of Joy* playing on the CD player when I killed him. I turned it up full volume to hide his screams and forever afterwards that goddamn song has haunted me.' He shrugs. 'As for twelve-o'clock, that was the time I killed my daddy and it became a habit. While the song was an omen, the time was a talisman.'

The sirens can no longer be ignored, and neither can the time.

Three minutes.

'Where are they?'

That's when he smiles.

Psychopaths like justice.

Particularly when it's poetic.

'She had it coming.'

'That accounts for Sally Kane,' I say, 'but what about the kid?'

A set of non-pneumatic tyres screech to a halt outside but the sicko's so carried away with himself that he seems unaware of it.

He shrugs.

'It's enough that she's your kid.'

Suddenly there's the sound of running footsteps outside. Grimaldi straightens the arm with the Luger in it. He's sighting me along the barrel so that all I can see is the little black hole that the bullet's supposed to come out of. His finger is whitening on the trigger as he's squeezing it, but the gat doesn't work because I took away the bullets during my little visit to 48 Daisy Drive. There's just this ragged click as I look away. That's when I notice the little red thing on the floor and that's when I realise it's the nose I gave Sally Kane all those aeons ago. The nose is telling me something that Sally Kane wants me to know, and that is their whereabouts – hers and Imogene's. I hear the echoes of the kid screaming on the ferris wheel and I realise those screams weren't ones of happiness but of dreadful fear. It wasn't just some kid, it was my kid, and she's heading the same way my sister Sophie went. I turn and beat it out through the door, nearly knocking into the two hoods, hobbled by the injuries I gave them at the farm but still able to move fast enough, especially when their quarry's sitting on the bed behind me. The handless one is screaming, 'Get out of my way, he's ours!' and the two of them are waving machine guns. In through the door burst the rozzers and they don't see me because the action by the bed is filling all of their sightlines. I'm already out the door and heading for the truck that Rory has about turned, leaping aboard as it takes off. The jokers on the back are starting to scream again and Salina and Goggle Eyes aren't all that calm either. Rory's yelling 'Where to?' to which I reply, 'The circus, you clown, the circus!'

Chapter 59

THE WHEEL OF DEATH

The flames have already taken hold as we round the corner, the core of the conflagration a screaming meteorite as death's wheel turns steadily on its axis. The bile rises to my throat and I'm a five-year-old boy again and my mother and sister are tied to the windmill. Only this time it isn't a windmill but a ferris wheel and it's no longer my mother and sister but Sally Kane and my only daughter, Imogene. It's no longer a hippy farm in Nimbin in the nineteen-sixties but a wombat farm in Dashiell in the first stages of the 21st century. I'm no longer a boy and yet somehow I still am, with it all happening all over again, and I feel myself cringe until something clicks inside me like the Luger that Grimaldi was wielding. Well before the truck lurches to a halt I'm out and my fedora goes flying and I jettison the gun and the coat comes off plus the shoes. It's like all the props and bells and whistles I've been relying on all these years have come off and I'm pounding past the joker at the controls of the ferris wheel wringing his hands and screaming, 'I can't stop the machine! Someone's done something to the machine!' I remember Sally Kane telling me her husband was some kind of mechanical genius. I realise that just like he fixed the Caddie he also attended to the machine after he'd tied Sally Kane and Imogene to it. He poured fuel into the bucket under them and set the fuse burning and the wheel turning with the STOP button neutralised so that nothing short of a gun blast could stop it. He then drove back to wait for me. The empty bucket in front of the one with Sally Kane and Imogene in it is rattling past, so I leap for it, my fingers grappling for a handhold as it spins me high in the air. When I look down I can see the bucket's already well alight and Imogene and Sally Kane are rearing back from the flames while Imogene's frightened, wide-open eyes are staring up at me. It's my sister's white scared face all over again and my sister's screams all over again, engulfed by flames all over again. But this time I grapple for the knots, and missing thumb or not I manage to get them untied. I feel Imogene's small body hot against mine and I'm gripping onto Sally Kane while Imogene's clutching onto me and the ground's rushing towards us as the bucket descends and I can hear someone yelling, 'Jump! Jump! Jump!' But I can't jump because the wheel's turning too fast. I make out a figure and it's Rory and he's swinging up his crutch to aim it at the engine and even above the roar of the flames I hear the detonation and at the same time feel the wheel lurch to a stop. The burning bucket sways close to the ground and it's only after I hit the dirt, my body hunched around Imogene to protect her, that I realise the person doing the screaming is me. Hands reach out and break my stranglehold on Sally Kane and get the kid's hands untangled from mine. As I fade in and out of consciousness I note that the people attending to Imogene are the hospital team from the float. I make sure the kid's okay and after that I limp around among the wombat droppings looking for Sally Kane, only I can't find her . . .

Chapter 60

THE RETURN OF
THE RED DWARF

The circus is a circus.

Whatever the do-gooders do, circuses are still circuses.

There might be no lions or tigers or elephants but there are still clowns and there's also still plenty of greasepaint, high wire and excitement.

Imogene was wary when I said I'd take her.

'You told me that before.'

'This time I mean it.'

'Didn't you mean it before?'

I lapse into silence.

Sometimes silence is the best thing to lapse into.

They kept us for observation, like they do, and then they let us go, like they also do. Imogene was just a bit shaken up and Sally Kane proved to be as tough as old rope. Salina was only suffering shock, but she's used to shock, and the hospital needed the beds, anyway. Sally Kane's paid what she owed and I've given most of it to Salina on condition that she let me keep Imogene another day. We've given the dead pooch a state funeral in a wombat hole, complete with a cross made out of the chair Salina was tied to. I can see the lights of the Big Top and hear the mutter of the generator and the shouts and screams of the kids having fun at the circus, only this time . . .

It's all over, I tell myself. Get a grip on yourself, Rainbow. So I do, at the same time as I take a grip on the crutch the hospital gave me, plus a grip on Imogene's paw, hard.

I focus on the signs.

They were flapping all over Main Street and dangling from gum trees, and hanging over the gate to the farm is the biggest sign of all, with trapeze artists smiling down from it and a ringmaster holding a whip, and in red and splashed across the sign like a spurt of blood, almost as an afterthought:

. . . and featuring, The Red Dwarf.

I feel Imogene's hand shake as we pass the ferris wheel, so I hold her mitt even harder, and also buy her a Triple-Blister Ice-Cream for distraction purposes.

Rory advised that he and Goggle Eyes would let us do the father-daughter thing but they would pick us up after, to drive us back to Sydney. But the ferris wheel's out of action due to the fire as well as Rory shooting up the engine and the fun in the Big Top hasn't started yet, so me and the kid are cruising down sideshow alley when we come to the rifle range.

'Can I have a turn, Daddy?'

The rifle's firing high but after I tuck the crutch under one arm and make the necessary adjustments and teach Imogene how to hold her breath and also how to keep the rifle as still as a rock and her eye on the target the way Rube taught me, she starts hitting most of what she needs to hit and also amassing a handy collection of kewpie dolls. I look over to see the flap of the Big Top closing.

'We better go in,' I say.

'Do we have to, Daddy?'

I think about that for a while and after thinking about it I tell her, No, we don't have to, because life's more than bread and circuses, life's doing what you feel you need to do at any given time and doing it often and doing the best you can under the circumstances. So Imogene goes on squeezing off the slugs and also goes on getting better and better at putting the slugs through the targets. Afterwards we tuck into a couple of big, sticky messes of red, yellow and blue fairy floss while the punters inside the Big Top are laughing and groaning and sighing like it's life on fast forward after a time warp.

'I like shooting guns,' Imogene informs me. 'Do you shoot guns a lot where you work, Daddy?'

I tell her, Yeah, I shoot guns a lot where I work.

'When I grow up,' she says, and here it comes, 'can I do what you do, Daddy?'

'It takes a lot of practice.'

'Does practice mean I get to shoot guns a lot?'

I tell her, Yeah, plus throwing people around and ducking and weaving and fighting bad people and rescuing damsels in distress, kind of thing, to which she replies,

'And rescuing boys, too?'

To which I tell her, Yeah, boys can be in distress, too. She seems to like the idea of saving boys in distress. By this time we're sitting on the plough that I'd tied the hoods to and we're watching the punters straggle out of the Big Top and Imogene's onto her fourth ice-cream when I feel the little body beside me go tense.

'Look at the little man!'

I look up to see a small joker coming out of the Big Top wearing a sugar-coated smile, clothes six times too big for his body, and hair you could cook a casserole on.

'It's just another midget.'

But I know it's not just another midget. It's a person that was too small to see out of his office window when Grimaldi took a pot at him, so that the bullets went over his head and the fall to the floor was a clown's ruse, making the porn merchant's report of the Dwarf's demise what might be called premature.

The Caddie's making its way past the blackened remains of the ferris wheel.

'Time to go, Sophie,' I tell Imogene.

Big pause.

Then, 'You were just joking when you called me Sophie then, weren't you, Daddy?'

I tell her, Yeah, I was just joking when I called her Sophie, but that doesn't mean she's not still gripping my hand hard as we climb aboard the Caddie.

Post-Mortem

A NIGHT AT THE SPEAKEASY

The speakeasy's doing it slow.

Hank's polishing the usual glass and gazing at the world through innocent eyes and a couple of stool pigeons are over by the Radiola offloading their hallucinations to a cop. A broad in an orange frock is wearing the dazed bright eyes of someone who's just shot up – and I don't mean lengthwise – and the pianola looks lonely. I carry my glass of aqua furiosa over to it, park the crutch, shift the controls to manual, spin the chair, lift the lid, and start hammering away at *Starlight*.

I forget the thumb and par consequence one or three notes find themselves in the Missing Persons Bureau, but you can adapt to anything in this world and so it is with *Starlight*.

Over by the bar I hear the Telefunken ring and Hank answer it.

I don't know what I expected when I took on the Sally Kane caper but it was never going to be a holiday in Bermuda.

Salina's taken a renewed interest in Imogene and Rory's busy converting Goggle Eyes – she's got a moniker, Janet – to his particular brand of religion while he's studying to become a minister. The hoods are back in jail where they belong and there was enough left of Grimaldi after the hoods had finished with him to join up the dots, crayon in the pretty picture and pack the remains back to the US of A to face the doh-se-doh.

Sally Kane's swapped Dashiell for Sydney, where she's doing a post-graduate course in psychopathology.

She's already done the practical.

'Play it again, Sam.'

Hank's so close I can identify his deodorant.

'The name's not Sam and it doesn't read that way in the movie.'

I sense him shrug.

'Have it your way, Rainbow. After all, you're the guy tickling the ivories.'

Hank's in one of his moods.

I'm playing it again when he interrupts again.

'By the way, I got a message from Rube.'

'So tell me the message.'

'She says quote unquote she's worked out what RED means.'

That makes one of us.

'And?'

'She says you got it wrong. The first letter isn't an R but a Q and the word's not a word but a bunch of initials.'

I put the music on Hold while Hank consults what he's written.

'That makes the initials – QED. Rube said you'd know what they mean.'

I know what they mean. They're the letters at the end of every chapter in the book Rube used to teach me geometry out of and as every kid that ever studied geometry knows, the letters stand for *Quod Erat Demonstrandum*, which is Latin for 'Therefore it's proven'.

The blonde guessed the truth and as the proof came up the hallway to kill her she had one thought in her head and that wasn't to identify the killer but to brag about how clever she was to her colleagues.

But I don't tell Hank that. Tell Hank that and I got more explaining to do than I need right at the moment.

So I turn my attention back to the music and after a while I hear Hank pad back to the bar.

That doesn't mean I'm alone.

Someone's standing behind me.

But I've had enough excitement for a couple of millennia so I give the joker the benefit of the doubtless and switch to Beethoven's *Ninth*. When I get to the bit with all the singing in it, the joker behind me starts in with the chorus.

The voice is familiar and by that I don't mean it's Enrico

Caruso or Benjamino Gigli or Joan Sutherland or even Carlo Begonzi.

I drop the lid, spin the stool, raise my peepers, and find myself face to face with Pandora.

About the Author

C.S. Boag is a former journalist who has also grown potatoes, driven taxis and bulldozers and worked in a hamburger bar. He has travelled many times throughout Australia and to France, speaking enough French not to die there. He was a Sydney City Councillor for six years and holds degrees from NSW and Sydney universities as well as postgraduate qualifications from Macquarie. Besides publishing short stories he has also worked as a columnist for *Woman's Day* and the *Bulletin*. He won the Walter Stone Memorial Prize for Literature in 1986. C.S. Boag lives on a small 'green' holding near Bathurst, NSW, with his wife, Judith. He has five children.

www.csboag.com

Also in the series

ISBN 978-1-922057-53-2 (digital)
ISBN 978-1-922057-54-9 (print)

ISBN 978-1-922057-67-9 (digital)
ISBN 978-1-922057-68-6 (print)

Published by Xoum in 2012
Reprinted in 2014

Xoum Publishing
PO Box Q324, QVB Post Office,
NSW 1230, Australia
www.xoum.com.au

ISBN 978-1-922057-45-7 (print)
ISBN 978-1-922057-20-4 (digital)

Cataloguing-in-publication data is available from the National Library of Australia

Word count 57,300